AF586446

A Cantraip of Tales

Contents

A Cantraip of Tales

Kennedy Smith

Introduction

SOFTLY as brown-eyed Angels rove
I will return to thy alcove,
And glide upon the night to thee,
Treading the shadows silently.[1]

There is something fascinating about the inexplicable, the unknown and we try our hearts out attempting to resolve things perplexing and mystifying. Perhaps I have tried in a way to promote such baffling through a lifetime of dabbling in the world of prestidigitation. The more I trifle, the more I realize what a vast unknown is out there waiting to be explored, to be dissected; for what alternative do we have? The human race has been and will forever be nosey.

---

[1] The Ghost - Charles Baudelaire

Here is a collection of trifles exploring the borders of my experiences or perhaps my imagination and there are times when my narrative escapes into the realms of fantasy. Some tales have some sort of basis in fact; others are purely fictional; and all have been embroidered to some extent. Perhaps memory flirts with the facts sometimes to fit the narrative or to embellish the yarn somewhat – so what. Who is a hundred per cent accurate with their account of events even with the best intentions?

I have called this collection of tales a Cantraip, an ancient Scottish word for spells. Is there an alternative collective word for such fables? There is no one set theme other than that of "The Unexplained" or "The Inexplicable" or "The Unusual". Or perhaps you do have a means for unravelling these happenings?

In any event, it is merely a look at some unusual circumstance which any of us could have encountered at some time or other, a collection of yarns, A Cantraip of Tales.

Chatterbox

'A bijou detached residence in open location in a quiet area with views of the nearby hills.' It is the estate agent's description of a house I once owned and it is roughly accurate. You could see the Ochil Hills (just) from an upstairs window but I'm not too sure what bijou means. What it didn't mention is that it was a house which talks. So what, says you! What's really damnable is that it didn't just talk during the day but all night too. Yackety-yak ... on and on. It's not as though it had any deep philosophical thoughts or statements at least at that stage; it was all just trivia ... the price of butter ... Tesco's special offers ... the local bus service.

The talking was not so noticeable during the day when the degree of background noise is high. Just occasionally during the long summer days, I noticed a murmuring conversation between the house and the local pigeons ... I wonder if they got fed up too? In the autumn, the trees get their own back by dropping loads of loudly-rustling leaves in the hope that the house shuts up and lets them sleep over winter ... well maybe not so much hope ... rather in revenge for their disturbed slumber.

I was first aware of this background conversation in the wee sma' hours last winter when I was awakened by a loud bang. Call me a coward if you like but I had no intention of leaving my cosy bed to investigate for fear of the unknown. It was then that I noticed this murmuring, this discussion as to the origin of the disturbance. At that time I put it all down my dreamy state but in the cold light of day, I began to wonder particularly as I could find no cause for the previous night's fright. As it happens, I did find out two days later when I noticed a picture was missing. The picture cord had parted and the picture had disappeared behind the settee. It shows how often I study my wall decoration! Perhaps the voices were just that ... voices in my head.

It was not long after that when I noticed moaning coming from the kitchen ... most disturbing. I had a good look around and finally concluded that it was emanating from the fridge-freezer during its defrosting cycle. Nevertheless, this moaning kept playing on my mind and each of these unusual happenings kept adding up.

Of course, all houses have their little idiosyncrasies ... timbers drying out, or indeed sucking up moisture ... water hammer in pipes ... mice in the attic ... birds perched on the TV aerial ... rattling windows in a wind ... that complaining door or groaning stair tread … and over time you get attuned to such characteristics. But voices! I'm sure I heard voices … or was it my tinnitus? For some time now I had been suffering … and I do mean suffering … from tinnitus of the hissing variety and this was affecting my hearing ability. The result was that I had taken to wearing a hearing aid. Perhaps it had been picking up radio signals from some local station. It could be; for any broadcast discussions I've heard recently seemed to concentrate on … well … the price of butter etc.

Then there was the sound akin to a snare drum. One night, I had just gone to bed after my shower and was just settling down with my latest acclaimed author, or so it said on the cover. There was a rat-tat-tat-tat, the staccato tapping. Ye gods! They've formed a dance band. No it wasn't; merely some residual water in the showerhead falling to the drip tray below. It's funny the tricks the mind can play!

What really clinched it for me was the night of the burglary. As I lay on top of the duvet one summer's night, I noticed some unusual noises from downstairs. The voices seemed louder than usual, indeed almost aggressive when suddenly there was this almighty scream and a sound of my outside door being wrenched open.

Outside there was a babbling of voices and it happened that a police patrol car was passing at that moment and caught this blubbing individual staggering from my house. "The place is haunted …" he kept repeating and he almost welcomed the presence of the law as they bundled him into the car. Apparently he had slipped the lock, entered my place but before he could nick anything he had been surrounded by these babbling 'things'. He got out promptly in a sort of panic.

That convinced me. The voices were not in my head; they were real. I decided to listen more carefully to these voices. What were the conversations going on all this time? Perhaps I might be able to join in and have a bit of fun.

After experimenting a bit, I found the sources for different conversations and even different accents … a most peculiar sensation! By sitting in different parts of my main living room, I caught these different variations. With a bit of experimenting I even tried joining in. "Excuse me." All went silent as the chattering stopped for a moment. "Excuse me! Do you mind if I take part in your discussions?" The silence continued.

I tried again. "What were you discussing?" The chattering started again just ignoring my intervention. A voice said, "Beyond them, I mean, beyond both brick and breeze." "Can I help?" I asked and a very posh voice responded, "And what do you know about it!"

I wasn't going to be fobbed off as easily as that; I tried to follow the gist of the conversation but it was away over my head. I'll try another area of the room and it was then that I noticed that the accents seemed to vary according to where I positioned myself. The nearer the centre of the house, the posher the accent! Now there was a conundrum for me to figure out. Why the different accents for different areas! Nearer the window I got to feel they (whoever 'they' were) were discussing different types of cement. "What happens in really frosty weather? I'll tell you. They put glycerol into the water but it's never really the same; the joint's just not the same."

I moved along a bit and the discussion there was about salt, not any old salt but the finely crystallised sort. "I tell you, it's face centred cubic. The crystal is known as a face centred cubic ... that's just the same as two cubes intersecting, a cube of sodium and a cube of chlorine atom ... that's what I said; face centred cubic." And so it went on. I felt out of that technical conversation so I didn't interfere.

What was it all about? I thought I would return to the more esoteric conversation and try to break into that once more. The conversation had moved on to the life beyond. What were they talking about, the afterlife? I tried to break in again but to no avail. They just ignored me. So I just went off and had my cocoa ... with a touch of rum, of course.

The following evening was just the same and indeed the different accents seemed centred in the same areas. I tried once more to break in but got a stern rebuke; "What do you want? Can't you keep your nose out of things?" There's no need to take that attitude, I thought. "I was just interested in your discussions," I retorted.

There was, what I thought, an embarrassed silence, but I think it was more of a stunned one. "We would like to continue this on our own. It's too personal for outsiders." I'm not an outsider, I thought. I live here. This is my house. I moved off to another area but they were still talking about chemistry and the reasons for the different colours of copper sulphate. Ah me, I sighed. It was no better elsewhere for they had passed from cement to concrete. And so the various conversations droned on.

I turned on the telly and turned up the sound.

The following evening, I tried a different tack. I thought that I'd play to their ego.

Back to the posh area.

"Hullo again," I ventured. "Tell me about yourselves."

"You mean that you have never heard of the Partition class of the world of Palisade. We are the ruling class here. Let me explain. There are three social strata in Palisade. There is Us, then Brick and finally there is Breeze ... in that order. Brick holds up the state structure with some help from Breeze. This is our World of Palisade."

I think I got the picture, so I thought that I would toss a spanner in the works. "What about Harle?" I asked. "Where do they fit in?"

"Harle? ... Harle? We know no Harle."

"Perhaps you know it better as Roughcast or even Render."

There was a pause. "Oh Render! They are a minority group. They don't matter." Oh yes!

I pondered that for a moment before resuming, "And what were you discussing to such lengths?"

"We were debating the possibility of life beyond Brick and Breeze. Perhaps you know more about that. You seem to leave this World of Palisade from time to time. You may even be able to shed some light on what happened before this World was created 44 years ago."

I reflected on this before continuing. "Well, outside there are many other worlds like this one and other social divides. You won't have heard of Stone or Chipboard or even Asbestos. I could go on and on and even describe the various wonders of the outside." I didn't dare mention Sod or Wattle for I doubt if their mind's eye could stretch that far. That seemed to satisfy Partition for the moment and conversation drifted on to other things.

Things wandered on like this for days ... weeks ... months. I was getting to know the voices better right across the social stratum. I even began to recognise the different voices and their little idiosyncrasies. To begin with, I did wonder where all their knowledge came from. I found out that, over the years they had developed a way of hacking into the memory banks of people but not into their data processing methods. We had little conversations about this and that, but I failed to find how they managed to speak or even how they managed to develop different accents.

On one occasion I was given an insight into their social setup. I was told by one lot – from the Partition crowd, needless to say – that the work was shared between the Breeze and the Brick lot whereas the Partition type supplied the aesthetic input, the shape of the rooms, their height and so on. Somehow I could sense an uneasy impression spreading from the others, the outside walls. "They do the work? What work?"

"Things such as holding up the roof, keeping draughts out … mainly the roof thing, though."

I had to be content with that for now.

In my interfering way, I tried to think of some way of bringing the various groups together. The nights were drawing in and we were really approaching the tail end of the year. Christmas was just round the corner and I thought – why not have a party to bring all together. I made such a suggestion to the Partition group and got the feeling of some sort of resent but grudging acceptance.

"Christmas? That's when I get lots of drawing pins stuck in me, isn't it?"

"That's for the special decorations we put up for the occasion. I have your agreement then? The other lot seem quite happy with the idea." There was further grumbling and muttering about pins. "OK. No pins then," and went looking for the Blue-tack.

The idea of a party looked like a good idea at the time but what sort of a party would it be. There would be no grub for a start, leastways not for them. We could sing carols but I didn't know if they could sing – must ask them. Party games? Well they would have to be of the mind-bending variety such as Scrabble; I think charades is out and certainly all the games involving dancing or movement such as Pass-the-parcel and In-and-out the Dusky Bluebells and most certainly Postman's Knock. I'll get some Christmas crackers although I reckon I'll have to wear all the hats and play with the usual rubbishy toys. Yet the jokes should be fun.

The eve of the Christmas party came to pass. The room was decorated in all its finery with the all-encroaching tinsel, stars, draperies and in the corner stood the traditional tree, lights all a-blinking. That dreadful noise was the sound of the various groups singing their own versions of Christmas carols. I had tried to teach them but it was a hopeless task and anyway they were trying – very trying.

I had decorated my coffee table for my celebration meal together with a holly-decorated napkin and Christmas crackers all in a row.

A glass of Tesco's best and we were off. To start with there was tomato soup, courtesy of Mr Heinz, with a little sprig of parsley. The frozen turkey dinner was next and the whole event topped by microwaved Christmas pudding and custard.

There were murmurings from my surroundings but no hint of after dinner speeches although I could sense there was an urge for Partition members to say something. "What happens now," came a bored voice? "When are we going to have a bit of fun, rave it up a little?" Somehow I had a little difficulty envisaging a rave. "Well, now come the games;" and out came the Scrabble board. It was the only thing I could think of where we could all take part other than telling tales ... maybe horror stories ... something like that. The Scrabble didn't go well. After explaining the rules, they proceeded to beat me every time not counting the time I cheated a little. We moved on.

"What about those other things on the table?" I had almost forgotten about the crackers. "Those are crackers. You grab one end ... of course you can't, can you. I'll tell you what I'll do. I'll jam one end into the door frame and pull the other like this." I pulled and the contents fell to the floor. There were various groans and sighs of boredom. "The winner gets to keep the contents. There's a paper hat and a little toy … " not much good to the Palisaders "and a joke of course or perhaps a riddle. This one asks: what did the scarf say to the hat?" For a moment there was silence. One Partitioner commented, "I didn't know scarves could talk." There was a snigger from a Bricky. "But it's a riddle … use your imagination!" I was getting exasperated by this time. "The answer is: You go on a head and I'll hang around, boom, boom."

There was a hint of a chuckle. I tried another. Bang … contents on floor … hat on head … plastic toy discarded and the riddle reads; "What starts with the letter t, is filled with t and ends in t?" Again there was silence. Still no reply. "It's a daft play on words. Come on, you were all good at Scrabble. Work out the answer! No? Well the answer is a teapot. Get it? Teapot starts with t … " Maybe the crackers weren't such a good idea after all. I'll try another.

Bang … hat … toy … riddle: "Why can't you be hungry in the desert?"

"Do you mean *desert* or *dessert?*" Murmurs all round.

"No! It says in this cracker *desert.*" I waited. "The answer is; because of the sand which is there … sandwiches there." Some chuckles from the Brick/Breeze side and after some deliberation, a Partitioner ventured, "But what about the Antarctic? It's a desert and there's no sand there."

At this, there were great sounds of derision and guffaws of laughter which grew and grew (which it does when you can no longer control yourself) as the Brick/Breeze lot hooted and shook with ridicule. The volume grew louder and louder and out of control. I could feel my ears crackling and all around a dusty haze formed and quivered and shuddered and rocked. There was a mighty crash as the kitchen ceiling gave up and came crashing down. This only served to spur on the roar till the very walls themselves seemed convulsed.

I could stand no more and rushed from the room, from the house itself and down into the street still wearing the paper hats. Even now the laughter followed me; the whole house rocked and shook. Fissures appeared along the harling sending showers into the street; the front wall crazed and swayed with the noise; shards of glass tumbled from the windows skewering the lawn followed by clouds of dust billowing from the empty frames; walls leaned outwards, too precarious; roof-tiles frisbeed to the side lawn. Inevitably gravity took over and the roof garrumped in on itself with a fog of dust obscuring everything. In the end, all cleared to reveal a jumble of brick, breeze block and jagged bones of wood. You could almost hear the silence.

I looked at the pyre of debris that was once my home, the end of the World of Palisade ... stared at Brick and Breeze and Partition in their death-throws, my friends and companions for the past while ... and mourned their passing.

Requiem in pace

For sale: A bijou pile of rubble in an open location in a quietish area with views of the nearby hills. Site ideal for redevelopment. What *does* bijou mean?

Velvet Face

Early in my professional career, I picked up this tale from an Indian friend of mine. In those days, Ceylon was called Ceylon before it became Sri Lanka. Some of the other place names may also have changed since then. Here then is the tale of Velvet Face as told to me in 1970.

***

My name is Sivakaraendarajah and I am a most respectable doctor in a town called Raka near Pottuvil in that most beautiful of islands, Ceylon. These days, I live in semiretirement all alone in my most beautiful villa on the outskirts of Raka where I can look out over the endless turquoise of the Indian Ocean. Occasionally, I enjoy a trip to nearby Pottuvil and sometimes as a special treat I even manage the journey to Kandy. It is all most tranquil, most peaceful, this life of leisure.

It was not always so though, for I started my practice in the waterfront region of Pottuvil. There, I built for myself a reputation far beyond my powers; for I used not only the medicine but also the psychology to treat my patients – a little foolish perhaps, but that is the prerogative of the young – and I was young. The annas flowed in and soon the rupees. Doctor Siva – they called me that – Doctor Siva was most successful.

During the third year of my stay in Pottuvil, there was a smallpox epidemic. In those days, such epidemics were not uncommon but one particular case stands out in my memory. This young boy was brought to my care in the height of this plague when everyone else was too busy to bother about psychological treatments. I call him a young boy. In actual fact he was about 18 years old, a Tamil from the north, with a name just as unpronounceable as my own. So, because of his slight stature and boyish ways, I called him Popni.

Now, Popni had got over the worst of the fever. Certainly, his eyes were still very large and his hair stiff with grease, but his main affliction was his rash which had now developed to the scab stage. We used the usual treatment of powders and ointments to relieve the irritation. Nevertheless he appeared disturbed, indeed, ripe for some of my psychology, for some Doctor Siva treatment.

One morning I approached him. "Popni, my little one, what ails thee?"

He blinked once or twice in wonderment before replying, "You know well, Doctor Siva. It is the smallpox."

"Ah yes, little one, but there is something else, something deeper, is there not?"

At this, Popni burst into tears and between the sobbing, his innermost fears and dreadings came out. He, the little Popni of the beautiful face, was to be shunned, stared at, because of his mass of smallpox scars. How very, very ridiculous all this is! Many people in Pottuvil were similarly scarred . . . there would be many more ... the Great Racha himself ... all to no avail. He was convinced he was a marked figure of scorn.

I worried over this through the heat of the day. A patient on the road to recovery should not be thinking the unhealthy thoughts. Yet, how could I lift his spirits! Certainly at that time I was conducting the experiments into rejuvenation of the skin using the special preparation – one of my own devising – an extract of the chestnuts and the ox bile. This was more in the realm of cosmetics rather than the medicine. Even so, here was an opportunity to try the balm under the most extreme circumstances.

I accosted my patient that evening. "Popni, my little one, I have an idea which will interest you and rid you of these scars that trouble your mind." He sat up with the alertness of a market mongrel. Here is a cream which will encourage your skin to renew itself and remain firm and young. Close your eyes, Popni, so that I can paint this cream to cover your sores, every one of them."

I applied the cream and taped a large piece of lint to cover the complete face apart from the eyes, the nose and the mouth. It happened that an essential part of the cure was heat treatment. The daily mask of cream was not enough; the skin had to be opened by heat. My idea was to use our wonderful Ceylon sun for this heat.

I devised a mask along the lines of a carnival false face covering the shape with black velvet. In this way, the heat of the sun would be absorbed by the black to give the desired sweating effect.

My little Popni looked quite fearsome that first day as he strolled out through the public throng with his black velvet face, an expressionless immobile face with only the large darting eyes to relieve it – rather, to enhance its weirdness. As I watched Popni leave my little hospital-come-dosshouse, people moved from his path, people turned to stare, people were afraid.

Popni continued his daily treatment, each day growing brighter in spirit. Actually, I think he was revelling in his anonymous role of Velvet Face. The peculiar face was such, now that he could not be recognised that he did not at all mind the stares of the people around him. Somehow, I think he felt the power of fear.

There came the day when Popni's treatment finished and although not perfect, the pockmarks were hardly visible. I was most pleased with the result and I think he was too; for he stood for many minutes admiring himself in the surgery mirror. "Look well, my Popni! The cure is completed. You can be normal again, my little one."

I watched Popni walk away from my surgery, hesitant at first but with greater confidence. No-one looked at him, no-one jeered, no-one feared. And soon he was jostled away from my sight by the endless throng, lost to me in that human sea forever ... or so I thought.

That evening, I was called out to a waterfront emergency. A man had fallen into the brown cess-water of the harbour and had been pulled out more dead than alive. He was calling for Doctor Siva.

With my bag in one hand, I pushed my way through the pressing crowd on my way to the scene of the accident. An acquaintance or two greeted me in passing, patients too; for I had much custom in that area. It took some time then, before I reached my new patient; not a new patient though ... an old victim. It was Popni. Fished from the filth of the harbour, he had not lasted long. He appeared to jump in, I was told . . . he took his own life . . . he wanted no rescue . . . jabber jabber jabber.

A hand touched my arm; it was old Radajah, a friend. "Before he died, he said he could stand it no longer. No-one looked at him, he said. No-one noticed him." I understood and nodded. Most ironic!

And yet on the way through the crowd, I thought I saw him – clutching something black in one hand.

THE MAN WHO SOUGHT RIDDLES

I first met David Stanford almost by accident while I was on a wild life project on the Island of North Uist, something to do with the nesting habits of the corncrake, as I recall. The day had started well enough. I had occasionally spoken to the locals about the little island off the west coast, the island with the giant white lump of quartz on the headland; they call it *Geal na Creag.* At the time I had the use of a wee seventeen foot boat, a Sea Nymph, with a 8hp Mariner outboard. I was just waiting for the right sea conditions to sail to and explore the island.

It was turning out to be one of those summers seldom experienced in the Hebrides; it seemed to go on forever and ever. The grass was parched crisp and the burns reduced to little more than a trickle. Even Talisker on Skye had to stop whiskey production in view of the water shortage; not I might say, to water-down their product but rather to cool their stills. Anyway, I prefer the Islay malt, Bruichladdich, but that's another story.

The corncrake that I was supposed to be observing had disappeared for the day and I felt it was time to have a closer look at *Geal na Creag.* I had plenty of fuel for the trip to the island and I duly left my cottage at Goular. As I motored round the bay and out by the point, I could feel the tide moving me south, so the journey to the island was taking longer than I thought. The boat was swept round and I made for a sandy shore ahead. In the lee of the island, I put out a stern anchor and waded to a convenient rock on the shore where I tied a stem line. At last I was ashore on my dream island; except it wasn't my island and that's what led to my first meeting with the real owner as I sat dreaming my time away.

My reverie was interrupted.

"Hoy; you there!"

Somewhat startled, I twisted round to behold a strange figure of a man. He peered at me through thick spectacles holding up an unkempt beard. The leather face was topped by a nondescript felt hat and the rest of his outfit betrayed an outdoor life. Somehow I sensed a feeling of guilt as I struggled to my feet and scrambled into my foot-ware.

"I . . . I was just going," I stuttered. "My boat's just over there." I could just detect his smile as he shook his head.

"I don't think so. The tide has dropped and your wee bit boat is high and dry. It'll be stuck for the next five hours. If you're landing here, best to gang round the heading. There is a creek of fair water where you'll be protected against all but a northerly. You'll ken the next time."

With that, he turned towards a sheltered bothy set over the shoulder of the hill and cooried against the elements by a few thrawn bushes.

On that first visit, I returned late essentially because I had to wait for the tide to release me. Dog tired, I returned to my cottage and fell into my bunk. I continued to feel the breathing of the sea beneath me and thoughts of the gentle downland of *Geal na Creag.* That night, the last thing I recall was my corncrake ward rasping me to sleep.

The following afternoon, my mouth told me it was time for a refreshing drink of some sort, so I made my way to *Balranald* camp site, the nearest thing to a pub, indeed the only place for miles around where the locals could have a quiet social refresher. My friend, Hamish had beaten me to it and had already sunk a couple of lagers. Glancing up, "A lager, Kenny?"

I nodded approval and sat with him on the bench.

"Did you get to your island, yesterday and find the magic white stone?"

"Nothing magical about it, just a lump of quartz; and . . . wait for it . . . and" pause "met the owner."

"You met Auld Davy! The Laird of *Geal na Creag.* What's he like then? Did you actually speak to him?

"Well, just to say 'hullo'. Do you know him, Hamish?"

"I don't actually know him, just that his name is Davy. He comes over from the island occasionally for provisions and the like. He collects his mail from the shop here and sometimes posts things." Hamish runs the post office here, among other things. "Apart from that, he doesn't communicate with us, not me or the others around here; so I don't really know anything about him."

I had a feeling that Hamish knew more than he was telling. If Davy collected mail, the post office was bound to know his full name but I didn't press the point.

"The sort of mail he gets is usually some sort of parcel," Hamish continued "and one time a parcel did 'accidently' break free of its brown paper. It was only some sort of book with a leather cover. It came from a shop in Glasgow; St Vincent Street."

I thought about this and wondered. "He lives in that old bothy? How does he manage to keep the mould from the leather? He would be better off with a Kindle of some sort."

"That old bothy, as you call it, is part of the original farm of the family who worked the island. It's quite large really – bigger that your cottage; much bigger. In any case, he doesn't have the electric so he couldn't recharge it."

Hamish and I went on to talk of other things and sink a few more cans. Anyway, night was closing in or what passed as night; for there was still a glimmer in the sky that far North. Bidding good night to my companion, I walked an uncertain way back to my cottage.

It must have been early morning and all was completely dark, well not completely; for there was a sky full of twinkling, the galaxies of the Universe. There were Mars and Venus brighter than the other heavenly bodies; the sweep of the vastness of the Milky Way. No smoke to spoil the impact on my mind. I gazed into space and there, the constellations gazed back.

The following day bloomed brightly with a gentle westerly breeze keeping the air cool. The corncrake showed itself briefly before chasing back to the long grass, no doubt to place another entry into its diary. About mid-morning the slight haze had cleared and my Stornaway tide tables showed that by 10am there would be a rising tide. This meant that the tide would be running from north to south with a maximum of around one knot, a mere nothing for those parts. I resolved to make another trip to *Geal na Creag.*

Dead on ten, I cast off from my mooring buoy and set course for the headland. Avoiding the large rocky island of *Trostrain,* I pointed the craft to *Geal na Creag* and sat back to enjoy the sensation of the sea. The gentle swell, the aftermath of the previous day, engendered a somewhat soporific awareness of my mind, not ideal for sailing and before I knew it, I was there.

Auld Davy had indicate that the safe haven was to the north of the island. I swung the head round and slowly meandered along the north coast and sure enough, there was an opening in the craggy shoreline. Making for this, I could feel the boat being gently sucked by the rising tide into a creek, quite narrow but soon to open into a calm lagoon.

The lagoon was quite an expanse of water with a sand beach at one end. The bones of a long-forgotten and half buried boat stared out at water wishing for one more voyage. Instead it had to make do with a flowery machair all around and not the sea. The yellows and the pinks, the blues and the purples reflected in the water. The ox-eyed daisies, the harebells, the red clover all spilled up over the foreshore to be stopped by a bank of heather, still to bloom fully. A gentle stream of fresh water meandered through the bed and leaked into the lagoon.

All along the rocks at the side were the rusty attempts of various mooring points. I tied a bow rope to one of the more reliable points and threw out a stern anchor to hold the boat from the rocks. With that, I cut the engine and clambered up the seaweed-slippery rocks.

As is my wont, I sat for a time on the sun-warmed heather and dreamed myself into the glory of the machair catching the perfumes of the wild flowers. Here and there I spotted some kind of wild orchid set in the middle of all this splendour. I could just sit here all day, I thought – but I was not destined for such.

"Ho there. I see you've found Paradise." It was the Laird. He had caught me in a dwam again. He must think I dream my life away – which I suppose I do. "I saw your boat on its way over – thought you were having some sort of difficulty when you didn't appear over the hill. I expect the aura of the place got to you."

I stood up in confusion and stuttered something.

"Come away up, if you can tear yourself away. That over-night rain has cleared the air and you can see for miles."

I clambered up the slope with some difficulty with the heather clutching at my legs and I tripped a couple of times and rolled in the soft heath. Wellies are not the best gear for scrambling. Reaching the Laird in some disorder, I muttered some sort of apology and stood there dripping sweat.

"Come on up to the top of the hill. The view is breathtaking in this light."

On he went, nimbly enough. I lagged behind in my heavy footware and after a bit, we reached the summit, me sweating profusely and puffing my lungs out, he fresh enough. He was right though. It was spectacular; the sea-green stretched out changing to a misty blue near the horizon with an occasional sparkle as the sun caught a breaking wave.

"See over there," and he pointed. "That's the St. Kilda islands group, *Hirta, Soay* and the rest. You can barely see them." He was right. I could barely see them. Just the same, I nodded. "Further round to the south; those islands are the *Heisker* group. You probably know them as *the Monach Islands."* He turned round. " And over there, of course, are the *Uists* and *Benbecula."*

It was only then that I noticed that was he no longer wearing spectacles. He must have caught my startled look and realised. "Och! The glasses are just for reading lad. I canna go on calling you lad."

"It's Kenny," I informed.

"Just call me Dave! The glasses? My eyesight is OK for most things since I had my cataracts done. I just wear the glasses for reading."

We both gazed at North Uist for a bit. Without any preamble Dave said: "You see those Islands over there?" I nodded. "They are the oldest rocks in the world, so I'm told." I reckoned he was old, but not that old and I glanced towards him. "Yes! When they were formed so many billion years ago, they were around about the region of the South Pole."

So much for that! We gazed in silence for a bit while the heat from the heather pushed me into dreamland again.

The Laird broke into my thoughts. "You're not from around here, Kenny?" He turned to me for an answer.

"No. No, I'm just here for a summer job. I'm doing a project on corncrakes, recording their habits and doing a sort of local census. Quite a task actually finding any. I do have one in the hay field next the cottage."

"Would that be Corncrake Cottage, then?" he asked. Seeing my puzzled look, he continued, "Yes, there really is a Corncrake cottage in that area."

For a moment, I thought he was taking the mickey, but no. "I didn't know that. Maybe I should concentrate my survey there."

We just sat for a bit and said nothing. I must say, he seemed a bit of an enigma and I was intrigued to find out more. Not that day for he abruptly rose and left without a word. The aura held me for a bit before I returned to my boat by way of a slide down the dry heather. The vessel was as I left it and I searched out my morning snack, a roll and a rather brown banana.

I seem to remember spending the rest of my visit, half in a dream, recalling the conversation with my new friend. Was he a friend and did I want to continue my rather uneasy friendship? At the same time, there was something deeper there even though our brief conversations were, to my mind, pretty superficial. I think I would like to find out more and make a return visit soon.

The following week was busy. My pal, the corncrake kept me on my toes with its comings and goings. Its nest, as I suspected, was in the long grass bordering the hay field and judging by the activity, its young had hatched and provided hungry mouths with ravenous appetites.

The evenings were spent with Hamish, my other pal. He was anxious to hear all about my second meeting with the Laird, but there was very little I could tell him. I certainly wasn't going to share Dave's thoughts on conservation. I did manage to screw from him the Laird's surname – the bold letters on the parcels. He was David Stanford, a vaguely familiar name; then again, perhaps that was all in my mind.

The evening was still and very hot with no breeze to cool the air. I think too that there was some degree of dampness there. Then it happened. A buzzing and the place was full of midges. I in my cottage bed (rather hard beneath) pulled the blankets over my head in an attempt to keep the blighters at bay. Landseer painted his famous Stag at Bay. He should have tried Midges at Bay.

A flash followed by rolling thunder broke the spell and the midges disappeared like magic as the building storm interrupted the still of the evening. Then I remembered, the name David Stanford was something to do with the supernatural or ghosts or something like that.

After that I slept soundly.

Perhaps the time has come for another visit to *Geal na Creag.* I was interested to find out why the Laird had isolated himself on such a remote island. The place must be rather short of ghosts, what with only one house there, as far as I could see. The forecast says it's going to be settled for a few more days and I think I can spare the time from my project. After all, it's not all that demanding. Mentioning my intentions to Hamish, he asked me to deliver two parcels (of books, probably) to the Laird since I was going that way. He gave me a sly little grin for he knew I was longing for a reason to visit the house on the island.

I set off next morning for that island with the parcel safely stowed. The crossing was unremarkable and I found the creek easily enough. As before, I found the scramble tough going up the heather bank as my sweat-lathered brow testified. Nearing the farm house peering at me with twin windows, I had a sense of anticipation mixed with a degree of foreboding. I knocked to a small shower of peeled paint. The door opened almost immediately and there was the Laird peering through his thick glasses, almost magnifying glasses.

"I noticed your boat about a half hour since. What kept you? Come in, come in laddie."

He took the two parcels and put them to one side. I placed my haversack on the floor.

“This’ll be my books from Glasgow.” He carefully removed the paper and placed the leather clad books on a small table. The wrapping paper was folded and carefully placed to one side.

I gazed round the room at the shelves of books, many of them similarly clad in leather and I could sense their tang. Even though they numbered around a couple of hundred, they seemed to have taken charge of the room and taken over the whole ambience of the space.

Noticing my interest, he said, ”These are my children, my riddles, my tales. I feel that there so much that these ancient books can tell us. You know, Kenny, these volumes hold a plethora of ancient knowledge now mostly forgotten. I search for these lost secrets, so far in vain. I’ll still continue my search till my last breath . . . fascinating work, you know.”

He then moved around the various shelves coming out with various book titles I had never before heard of, nor did I understand.

“Somewhere in these ancient books lie all the riddles of life, if only I could solve them; the riddles of life and death and what lies in wait in our futures. You know, Kenny, this small collection holds all the answers. I just haven't managed to find them – not yet. Some day."

"Are these tales of ghosts and things?" I asked

"Oh! You've seen that stupid TV programme. That was some time ago; and anyway, they completely misinterpreted what I was trying to explain. All they could think of was ghosts, ghosts, ghosts. It had nothing to do with ghosts, not really . . ." His voice tailed off, a trifle despairingly.

I wandered around looking at the spines of the various books. I was still no wiser. I'm sure there must be some way of cataloguing these tomes, say electronic, to make it easier to access their secrets.

"Don't you have an e-book?" I asked

"Eh?"

"An electronic book, a Kindle?" I explained

"No! I like real books, ones that I can feel in my hands whether it be pulp, fine paper or parchment-like stuff. I like to twist back their soft jackets till the spine splits; or let their hard, glossy covers slip through my fingers; I covet the chance to feel the luxury of the leather of ancient works."

"It would be easier to extract the information if it were stored electronically" I explained.

"You don't understand, Kenny. Books have an odour, a smell of printing ink when new, that dusty reek when rediscovered on your shelf and even last night's guff from a fry-up. There is some errant marmalade sticking together pages 58 and 59, a reflection of a steamy passage. I like to look at them with their lurid dust covers, trying to out-guess their story before I've even looked at a word. They lie about my house as ornaments waiting to be tidied away – but I'm still reading that – squeezed into a bookshelf where they assume a coating of dust over time; or even – but rarely – catalogued and never through electronics." He sighed as to say, 'These youngsters!'

He continued his diatribe: "You can take them anywhere; the sandy beach midst salty air; a steamy bath for an hour at a time; even to bed without any peripheral demands only to waken to the sound of it hitting the floor. Paperbacks live their lives travelling in pockets, in handbags, brief cases, perhaps even held between teeth while you look for your bus change; or sometimes accidentally left behind on the seat of a train. They have exceedingly adventurous lives and when their time has come and they have been read, they serve to prop up a wobbly table or suchlike. I once had a great thick tome which was even musical in a sort of a way. I used it as a footstool for my left foot when playing my guitar."

"You play the guitar?" I asked. I had seen what looked like a violin half-hiding in the shadows.

"Not any longer. The hands are just not up to playing. That bump on my index finger prevents me from using a *barré*." So I have to rely on my books for my pleasure. "

"Of course, you can use a book for more than just reading. It's really quite a versatile thing. You can throw a book at the odd mouse – or even the odd rent man or debt collector. Who needs a bookmark when you can dog ear your place, unsightly as it seems. Those of us of a mischievous frame of mind can tear the penultimate page from your latest who-dun-it and pass the volume on to someone you don't much care for. BUT - never, never destroy a book, Kenny! That is the end of civilisation."

"I hadn't really thought about it that deeply," I admitted. "I suppose most folk have a scattering of books lying about their homes."

"Not a bit of it," he retorted. "You'd be surprised how neglected the printed word is. Even newspapers are having a hard time now that instant news is available through TV. There was a time when every stately home had its library. Often it was a retreat for the master of the house complete with his tantalus of three drinks, whiskey, malt and port. It was convenient for Agatha Christie to dump her murder victims there – in her literary sense. There was always a safe behind an out-dated encyclopaedia and the whole room had a miasma of tanned leather and stale alcohol. All good stately piles should have one. As you can see, my library is a very make-shift affair with books crammed in at all angles. On top there are piles more, all spines out with the mother-in-law's photograph perched there to boot."

I didn't like to agree with him but his shelves did look a bit chaotic. No doubt he knew what was where but I did wonder.

"I've always liked books ever since I was a kid," he continued. "Then, my favourites all had pictures. Now they conjure up mind pictures, in vivid colour even and there are times when I can imagine perfumes, the tang of the hills, the stench of a cesspool. Some writers recognise this; they make the page live; they make you feel you are actually there. You get anxious over their victims. You identify with the heroes. You anticipate the baddies' sticky end. You live all their experiences." He was quite carried away by this time. Obviously books meant a lot to him and his search for this elusive jewel occupied his very life.

"A book is a parallel universe with exploding supernovae, their galaxies, Greek gods and goddesses, planets, orbits, meteorites, asteroids and all the various celestial paraphernalia. It is a cosmos which can be closed away at a moment's notice as you slam it shut and later brought back to life again. The tale is just as you left it. It's like a conjuring trick with a minimal degree of sleight of hand. Just open the book!"

"I only asked if you had a Kindle!"

"Aye, Kenny. You can see I get carried away at times. Do you fancy a cup of tea. I'll put on the kettle."

"I've brought some food with me," indicating my haversack. I lifted out my packet of rolls and my knot of bananas. I noticed a sudden spark of interest.

"Ah, morning rolls! I don't see such delights in my little island home – and bananas too."

So together we had our modest meal in the little library on a makeshift table cleared of its crop of books and talked of many things. Time past and my watch indicated that I should be off if I were to catch the falling tide and return to North Uist.

"Come again Kenny and perhaps we can put the World to right."

I grinned my farewell and slid down the heather bank to my wee boat.

Two days later I returned to the island bearing gifts of more fruit. I guessed that Dave was missing his vitamin C and his morning rolls. I approached the house in the hollow as before and was greeted by somewhat preoccupied Laird.

"Come in, come in Kenny and take a look at this." On his table he had an ancient volume spread wide at one of its illustrations. The printing on the page was in some sort of Gothic script, not my cup of tea. Nevertheless, I looked and nodded sagely even though it meant nothing.

"This is an old book from Saxony, probably from Dresden;" He pointed to a particular passage, "and here is a reference to Michael Scot."

I nodded and continued to be dumbfounded. What was all the fuss about? The name meant nothing to me. "So who's Michael Scot?" I asked.

He was one of the great intellectuals of the 13th century. He came originally from the south of Scotland and was well sought after by the courts of Europe. It is said he was a magician, but I wouldn't know about that. It is a lead, just the same. I must sit down and try to translate this section to see if it leads anywhere."

I was a little bit uneasy about things magical. "Is it about black magic then?" I didn't really want to know.

"No, no! Nothing like that, but Scot wrote some very erudite papers. I just haven't been able to locate any. Not that I could afford to buy them for they would all be handwritten – pre-Caxton, you know."

I didn't know.

"There are sure to be later copies of his work, even press printed ones. I haven't found any of those either. This might be a lead, though."

I was late leaving the haven of *Camas Lurach.*

The state of the sea had changed. A heavy swell had developed from the west, the legacy of some distant Atlantic storm and for a time it was quite exciting climbing slowly out of the trough and surfing rapidly into the next one. After a time, it began to feel quite sinister and my thoughts returned to the Blue Men of the Minch. To complicate things, a mist stated to form and in no time I could hardly see the bow of the boat, so thick was the cloud. Now, where was that horn, the one worked by a can of compressed CO_2? It should be somewhere in the cockpit locker. By the time I had found it, the boat had careered off course, almost parallel with the swell. Checking this with the compass to 90º East, I could feel some degree of panic before I returned to the normal course. Indeed, the circumstances were not normal. With no sight of land, I should be playing it safe to a more northerly direction and duly changed to 45ºNE and lookout for *Trostrain* that rock just off my home bay. Yet, I didn't want to go too far north and get caught in current through the Sound of Harris. It would be strong at this state of the tide – and there would likely be commercial traffic running there.

By this time, I should be nearing the coastline, so I cut the engine and listened for the sound of waves breaking. Nothing. Just the silence of mist pressing in, the reflection of the navigation lights, the heaving bosom of the Atlantic swell! With a toot of my fog horn, I restart my engine and continued to feel my way shoreward.

A shadow passed my line of sight. It is a seagull just as lost as me. I should be really close to the shore now. I cut the engine again and I think I can hear waves breaking. Peering over the side, I see no bottom, no rocks, no sand. Seaweed drifted by indicating rocks rather than sand so I cut the engine to a whisper. The mist darkened and quickly changed to a looming cliff, a characteristic unfamiliar to that part of the coast. The heat of the land is clearing the mist and away to the SE I recognise the gathering of tents at the campsite. The compensation to my usual course has taken me too far North. I gratefully swing the boat round and turn up the engine. The cliffs must have been those at *Rubha Dubh.*

Back at the mooring I have a profound sense of relief. I can feel my hands shaking as I tie-up. Back at the cottage, I finish off the last of my bottle of *Bruichladdich.*

The following week took me off to the mainland on bird business. I missed the end of the warm spell and the weather closed in by my return preventing a return visit to *Geal na Creag.* I did try, for in the afternoon, it seemed to moderate a little, enough to turn my thoughts to taking my boat out to *Geal na Creag.* It was calm enough in the bay but as soon as I cleared the headland, the seas swung the head of the boat round so that I was broadside to the wind. A vicious gust rolled the boat over on its side causing sea to pour into the cockpit. No! This was no sort of weather for my wee bit boat. I returned to my mooring pumping out all the while.

The following day certainly promised much with sunshine and a greatly reduced wind. It was still blowing from the west but had lost much of its ferocity. I prepared Anda, the boat with additional fuel for the journey and packed a selection of fruit for the visit.

As ever, the engine started first pull and we made for the headland with the oilskins at the ready. Even in the shelter for the bay, I could feel a considerable swell, the legacy of the storm. Rounding the headland of Trostain, the little boat met the full force of the Atlantic swell with the white tops spraying over the bow. Time for the waterproofs. Even the act of rigging my clothing with my hands off the wheel was enough to let the bow swing round and turn the boat broadside to the wind. I quickly swung Anda on course before the next wave hit. Up to the crest and down into the trough was the pattern. Sometimes cresting a wave would cause the propeller to leave the water and race, the boat would lose steerage and swing to starboard before relenting and returning to course. I managed to correct this by taking an angle to the crest.

This was hard work for the wee vessel and we made slow progress. If anything, the wind was increasing as we left the mainland and spray was blowing from the tops. There were times too when the head dug in and great water sprouts would rear and throw their wet arms around us. I worked hard pumping out.

The sea now was reduced to a finer chop with the frequency of the waves lessoned to an uncomfortable lumpy state and a higher spume over the windscreen. I crouched down to avoid the sting of the spray and gazed at the blurred view through the screen. Great spouts shot up and fell against us in jets of green and I was conscious of the rigging's high-pitched scream and the machinegun slap of the stern flag.

All at once, I was aware of a dark shape ahead. More by good luck than navigation it was *Geal na Creag.*

By habit, I took a course around the north coast of the island, but one look at the creek ruled out that as my harbour for that day. The boisterous sea running past its entrance and the swell within decided that. I turned our head round and headed for the sheltered south bay and its sandy shore. There, I dropped a stern anchor and took a line ashore to a tying-up point there. That part of my ordeal was over.

I scrambled up the slope to the Laird's home half expecting to see him standing in its doorway. No David. I would not be expected in view of the weather or perhaps he had just missed me in the poor visibility. A knock on the door produced no reaction or sound from within and with some trepidation, I opened up and entered.

I knew straight away that the place was empty; it had that distinctively empty feeling. There was no *Marie Celeste* about it – no abandoned meal – no litter of papers – just nobody. Indeed all indications were that the evacuation had been quite orderly and planned; for not only were all Dave's personal effect gone, so also were his collection of ancient books.

I sat there and looked around uncomprehendingly. What had prompted such a sudden exodus? Seeking an explanation, I sat there munching one of my bananas; food helps me think. There was a folded sheet of paper on his table which, up till then I had ignored in my haste and shock. It had my name on it. I opened the paper; it said simply:

Dear Kenneth – my name is Kennedy not Kenneth

I have decided that I cannot spend another winter on my island home. It rather loses its glamour in the sort of winters we have here and the opportunity arose to have my books transported by fishing boat back to the mainland. My intention is to move to my place in Doune in Stirlingshire and continue my researching there.

I wish you every success in your future studies in Glasgow.

Yours sincerely,

David

There was a Doune address and a telephone number.

Still deep in thought, I pushed off and back into a lively sea. The nature of the waves had changed again to a shorter frequency and longer wavelength. What should have been a thrilling return journey was lost in thoughts about my friend's abrupt departure. The boat would climb to the crest of a wave followed by a swift surf down its steep slope to meet the next rise. The result was a faster than anticipated approach to the home shore and I had to backtrack into the waves to travel further north to the opening to my home bay and its shelter.

Mooring the vessel and the trek back to the cottage continued in this vein, this half-dream world. I don't know what I was worried about. Davey had decided to leave his island and a convenient chance transport had come along and he had seized it. That was all.

Later that week, I packed my few belongings, said my farewells and left complete with my obligatory sprig of heather to remind me of these times. My contract with the corncrakes had expired.

I was getting a taste for this book-collecting lark. I had been to a few auctions and I had already collected a few of my own but nothing compared to Davey's collection. I have nothing remarkable although I do have a rare Scottish Jamieson Dictionary from 1866. I keep my eyes open and attend many an auction in the hope of picking up something rare. Apart from the dictionary, this has still to be realised.

About two months later, I had arranged to meet David Stanford in a café just off Sauchiehall Street. I told him all about my latest interest, an interest in old books and he gave a wry little smile. "So you're hooked are you? I thought it would get you in the end."

I went on to tell him about some recent purchases including the dictionary and he nodded here and there. In a pause, he intervened with "While waiting to cross Hope Street in Glasgow, I bumped into Lynn Fennel, an auctioneering acquaintance. You may know her. She knew of my passion for books, for I had traded with her several times for some minor little items. After the usual remarks about the weather (unusually sunny for this time of year) she moved on. Then she told me that there was to be a house clearance in the Inverness area on the 27th and there would be quite a collection of books going. That brightened up my day more than the sun – us bookworms tend to be shy of bright days – and I noted details of the presale day. I said I would endeavour to be there."

He could see that I was interested. "Would you care to come along? It'll be useful experience and you might even see some thing that appeals to you."

I hesitated. "Inverness, you say?"

"Yes, near Inverness. I'll give you a lift there and we'll probably have to spend the night, so bring an overnight bag," Dave added.

That was that – all arranged.

It turned out that the house to be cleared was on the East side of Loch Ness - the side that tourists seldom see - about halfway along and had once belonged to a pop star. Moreover, there were rumours that occult happenings had been rife in the establishment but I just put that down to hearsay. Nevertheless, it made me wonder what sort of books would be in the sale. I'm not into the supernatural.

When the viewing day arrived, we prepared for the long drive North with a pack of sandwiches and several cans of Coke. Having decided to take the West route rather than the dreich A9, we started early ... up through Crianlarich, Tyndrum and Glen Coe ...

across Ballachulish to Fort William and hence to Fort Augustus where we took the right turn to take us along the East side of Loch Ness. We had booked in for two nights in a small hotel in nearby Foyers.

The Highlander was much like any other small Highland hotel with big aspirations. It had six bedrooms and a dining area butting onto the bar area also open to the locals. After a passable evening meal, we sat at the bar looking at a fair collection of single malt whiskeys mainly of the Speyside variety with an occasional Islay. I decided on a Bruichladdich and looked around the bar area ... only one other, a local I guessed.

After a time (and another Bruichladdich) the landlord wiped his way along the counter and ventured, "You'll be here to see the big hoose, then?" and seeing my puzzled look added, "Aberlenie Hoose." I nodded. "Have a dram," I reluctantly offered. "Do you know the place? We thought we'd have a look at the sale."

"Oh, the place has been empty this long stretch ever since they lads went. Some wild nights ah can tell ye and strange sounds too."

"Yes, they were a pop group isn't that so?"

"Och, I'm no' talking about the playing although that was queer enough. Naw naw! I'm talking about other things ... screeching and yellin' and oh the wailing. It wasn't a place I'd go near of a night, ah can tell ye." He moved off further down the bar to serve the other customer and the two of them sidled up to us.

"Donald here was telling me that he has passed the Big Hoose of a night and seen some terrible sights ... all sorts of caterwauling too ... "

Donald joined in; "There was a time last midsummer; there was still a glimmer of light in the sky so I wasna' feart or anything. There was a 'thing' walked through the outer palisade of the front terrace ... didn't wait to see any more," and the two of them slid away to the far end of the bar. I think I heard a muffled giggle but I couldn't be sure. I feel they were just having us on and it didn't bother me; for we were just going along – in daylight – to Aberlenie house to find out what they had in the way of books, not ghosts.

That night lying in bed I got to thinking of their hints of ghoulish apparitions as the September wind whispered round the eves of the house giving a suspicion of a rattle at the window. There crept over me an apprehension, an angst. What could there be within the shell of the old house. After all, that pop group had lived and made merry there for many a day without catastrophe. Or had they? I had a vague feeling that the group had broken up over some stroke of bad fortune.

The following day, we motored over to Aberlenie four miles or so and came across the gaunt grey building around a sudden bend in the road. I was half expecting extensive estate grounds but there it was almost overlooking the roadway. There was another car parked there when we arrived for it was just after the onset of the viewing.

Inside, the caretaker (I assumed) was bustling around pretending to look busy. "You're early, first I think. Just have a look around; there are some catalogues over there next to Venus de Milo." She wasn't exactly pointing the way but I readily found the record and some approximate prices indicated. It would be my guide on affordable items (to me, that is) and I duly produced a pencil and started marking certain items. Dave was having a good look at his catalogue, no doubt searching for ancient books.

Moving from one musty room to another, we soon jaloused the layout and presently made our way to my main interest, the library. Having cleared a dusty table, we selected a few choice items and started to flick through their pages looking mainly at the frontispiece. That is where the value lay.

"Have you found anything of interest, Dave?" I asked.

"I'm looking for items that fall within my interest and there are certainly some very old volumes here but they seem to lean towards the occult, not really my interest. What a pity for they had beautiful leather bindings, soft and alluring and enticing with a certain magnetism possessed by ancient craftwork. However, value was not my guiding light; I looked for pieces that fell within my interest.

"Hullo there, David, Ken! I thought I'd find you two here." It was Lynn keeping an eye on the prospective interest in the sale.

"You'll be taking the auction then?" I asked.

"Yes; anyway for part of the time. We have some problems, though. I can't get a reliable internet signal as we move from room to room. There should be a number of interested buyers out there. I have managed to rig some landlines but the signal within the building is dicey to say the least ... worse than useless." Oh, I thought; less competition for my interests.

Off she went with her problems and I resumed my search with revised interest; I might be able to pick up something of a bargain in view of the reduced competition. So, back to the more desirable leather bound volumes.

Many of the volumes were individually priced in the catalogue, so I could guess that these would be greatly in demand. Indeed, Lynn Fennel might be bidding for some private client and that would keep the prices up. Here was an old leather-bound volume not on the list, though ... *Altera Rationem ... 1566 ... R. MacKenzie.* The leather was a rich reddish-brown and well polished through countless eager hands. Looking inside, I could see the title repeated and in smaller letter below ... *Rector Siderum Cognitione* ... all in carefully illuminated letters, red, yellow and black. Strange it wasn't in the catalogue.

"This is an interesting volume, David, but it's not in the catalogue."

Dave shuffled round to have look. "Yes, there it is ... Hand written copy of a 13th century book by Michael Scot together with three pewter items ... If you look on the second page, you'll see the details there. . . " His voiced tailed off.

Sure enough, there it was:

Altera Rationem
Rector Siderum Cognitione
Michael Scotus
AD 1203
Astrologus in Atrio Frederick II
Ex Sicilia

Exscipta by Robert MacKenzie
AD 1566

Yes there it was, although I didn't fancy the pewter ware a lot. Estimated price between £150 to £600. Quite a range! The work was in Latin throughout so I had some difficulty deciphering the contents. It seemed to be about the stars for there were various celestial maps and references to *planate Veneris* and *Iovis planetae.* It would be interesting to see the views on astronomy and compare these with present day knowledge. On the other hand, David was much more interested; indeed he was quite excited to the extent that he pencilled it on his catalogue.

The auction had already started when we arrived the following day ... too much Bruichladdich the night before. It didn't really matter for they had not yet reached the library stuff. Indeed, it was into the afternoon when Lynn started on the items we had ear marked. I got a bundle of Victorian Game Books for a knockdown price. I don't really know why I bought them – a record of Donald M. MacKenzie's grouse killing days. I suspect the fine leather bindings enticed me. I'll probably sell them on.

"Lot 3150; a fine reproduction of an early 13th century book, circa 1566, together with some pewter ware," ... Dave got in early with £150, and after some desultory bidding from the opposition, finally took the honours with £210 (plus commission.) We settled up around 5pm and set off with our purchases. It was only later that we found we had 'accidently' left behind the pewter items.

It seemed an eternity before we arrived back and I could see that David could hardly wait to examine his recent acquisition. Clutching his leather covered tome, he dropped me off in Glasgow and hurried home muttering something like "See you . . ."

It was some days before I heard from The Laird – I still thought of him as The Laird – a rather breathless phone call. "I've been having a good look through my *Altera Rationem by Scotus.* I tried to get the gist of the contents. I suppose the original would be on velum or parchment; this was simply on ancient paper, becoming rather fragile and faded to a crisp brown. I'm afraid I made a rather fundamental mistake though. In the title it said *astrologus* and not *astronomia* ... astrology not astronomy. In my haste to acquire the volume I had bought a book which was outside my range of interests. In spite of all that, I was determined to make the best of things to stick to my task of getting a rough idea of the contents."

He went on further; "The first part was all about the current position of the stars ... *in firmamento ... Iovis Etiam in aeri* ... and the effects on the affairs of the King of Sicily. Skipping to the next section revealed lots of what I took to be mathematical formulae ... *mathematicas deducuntur* ... away above my head. This developed into a discussion about ... *quatuor dimensionum ...* the fourth dimension which was what the title suggested. Now, what was all that about!"

I could hardly get a word in as he continued; "I picked out parts here and there to get a flavour of the discussion. One section caught my eye for it mentioned a part of the borders of Scotland not familiar to me. Although I had visited Melrose in the recent past, the allusion to Eildon was unfamiliar. In this section, he says because of the Zodiac ... *virtute magna creata est ...* great power was created. He says he used the Zodiac wheel in order to enter the hollow hill of Eildon and there he did ... *per usura is est potential perdere malo* ... destroyed the evil place using this power. In its place there are now three hills of Eildon ... *collibus tria Eildon."*

"In the previous section there had been some detailed discussion on the manipulation of the 'Zodiac Wheel' but I had skipped over these details as being too laborious to work on. Perhaps I'll have a closer look at this section. It is illustrated by a Zodiac mosaic that he had copied during a visit to Rome and beautifully copied into this version by Robert MacKenzie."

"Can you manage to come over to Doune, Kenny and we can discuss the various implications of the various sections. I'm free on Thursday."

How could I refuse?

I arrived early in Doune in anticipation of an interesting day. They always were with Davey at the helm. He was all excited and greeted me like an excited schoolboy. "It's all to do with a code letting Scot enter another world, a forth dimension, he calls it. I'm missing one thing. Really, I've left something behind."

Seeing my puzzled look, he added, "The pewter ware from the auction." He dragged me into his study and pointed to the relevant text. The detailed instructions did not mean a lot until Scot mentioned the grey disc with the markings ... *discus stria cano picturas.* A grey disc? Could that be the pewter plate, the plate that I had stupidly left behind at Aberlenie House?"

He flicked the pages over and pointed to a section. "Now the instructions are beginning to make sense. They refer to the various signs of the Zodiac. Apparently, these signs are on the large pewter plate, the one I left behind. So far in my struggles with the translation, the instructions direct that you stand in the centre of the plate facing *Pisces.* Mark the position of *Pisces* with the jug as a reference point. Then place one foot, the left one, on *Capricorn* and the right one on *Taurus.* Slowly trace the left foot along the arc till it rests on *Aries.* Cross the right leg behind the other to rest on *Pisces* so that you are now facing in the opposite direction. Trace the left foot along the arc till it reaches *Gemini* ... and so on through several of these orders until the final command – place both feet in the centre."

"He then goes on to warn ...*cave virtute discus...* beware of the power of the disc followed by further descriptions of matters related to the Hill of Eildon, the tremendous energy, the white heat within the hollow Braes of Eildon; enough energy to melt rocks, to send boiling plasma into the atmosphere. He described further phenomena of frightening energy and upheaval finally ending with ... and in the end there were three Hills of Eildon."

"As far as I could follow, he puts the fountain of this great power down to the disc itself. He describes how he forged the item from some ore discovered on one of the Orkney Islands. What developed was a long discourse on the alchemy involved, all very complex and incomprehensible, at least to me. He describes the peculiar glowing appearance of the Orkney material ... *viridi fluorescens* ... and the thrill he encountered when he touched the material. He had several workers processing the raw material treating it as though they were making iron. He also mentioned that some of the men fell ill during this process and died shortly after. He put this down to poisoning. Anyway a thin disc of this material was cast and he noted that it buckled slightly on cooling. That corresponded to my 'pewter' dish. So these pewter items all seemed to be part of the same artefact – and the dishes part is still at Aberlenie House."

The auction was almost three weeks in the past. We had to do something quickly or lose some essential prop for all this magic mumbo jumbo.

Dave made a quick call to the Highlander to establish the whereabouts of house caretaker and how to contact him. No problem! He got Hugh MacFarlane, the caretaker, straight away and explained that he had 'accidentally' left some items behind. "Well, there's been no one in the house since the auction so it'll be safe enough. I'm in the cottage just up the road from the big house; a wee white house with green windows. Ye canna miss it." Dave said he would be up at the weekend and left it at that.

"I'm sorry, Dave, but I'm tied up this weekend," I told him.

So David had to go off on his own to collect the bits and pieces. Later he told me just what had happened at Aberlenie House. The story he told seemed crazy and out of this World – literally – and I found the whole thing unbelievable.

This is what he reported in his own words:

The weekend came and I set off on the Friday night intending to stay again at the Highlander. I had brought my translation notes with me together with some cleaning fluid to remove the grime from the dish.

"So you're back again are you ... couldn't keep away?" I was greeted by the landlord. He had an extended grin on his face; I guessed that he had shared some private joke with his regular, Donald, at my expense.

"Yes. I left behind some things at Aberlenie House after the auction," I explained. "I'll collect them in the morning."

"Aye! I certainly wouldn't venture up there in the dark." Night had long fallen for we were well into October and I was inclined to agree. "There have been tales of strange lights about the place."

Accordingly, I contented myself by sipping Islay malt to pass the evening and plan in my mind my programme for the following day.

The Saturday was bleak with low grey cloud threatening the air with large rain dollops. A cold wind from the distant North Sea cut me right to the marrow, a great beginning to the day. I found the little white cottage with the green windows with no problem and the caretaker recognised me from the auction day. He handed me the key to Aberlenie House adding that there would be no power or water. "Just drop in the key on your way back," and left me to it. I thought he might have come with me just out of curiosity. I would have appreciated the company.

There was nothing for it; I was on my own, a large key in one hand and an LED torch in the other. The heavy door opened without a hitch but true to all horror stories, it did protest somewhat with squeals and a high-pitched rasping sound. As I entered the dim interior, the extreme cold hit me together with a sensation of musk. I shivered. As I made my way to the library, I noticed a strange happening. My torch looked as though it was glowing spontaneously. My mind playing tricks! There at the far end of the room were my pewter items as I left them. They probably would have lain there for all eternity but for my return.

I played my torch over the items – yes, they had the dust and grime of centuries forming an unsightly coat. Must get my bucket and some water and scrub the artefacts. There should be no shortage of water in these parts yet it took some time before I found a water butt next an outhouse.

Scrubbing brush and 'Multipurpose' cleaner failed to reveal any symbols or signs on the dish; the same with the jug and a smaller cup-thing. I tried moving the disc nearer the window and the remains of the daylight. It was then that I discovered the great weight of the dish. It must be of lead. Looking at it closer, I tried to scratch the surface with my penknife to no effect. Were it lead, it would have marked quite easily, but no. It was really hard.

The disc was only about two feet across and yet it was only with great difficulty that I managed to get it up on edge and roll it nearer the window where I let it fall with a great clatter face-down on the bare floor. There around the little dome were the Zodiac ciphers cast into the structure, thus

I had been looking at the wrong side of the disc.

Anxious to get started, I fetched my notes and the jug, attached the torch to my headband and stood on top of the dome. Then began my macabre ritual, facing the jug and Pisces, *one foot on* Capricorn *the other on* Taurus, *I twisted round through the sequence, back and forth, forth and back in a grim minuet. This was not a dance; this was a concoction like a safe combination. It was for opening a door ... to where? At the limit of the routine, I hesitated before the final move. Then it was done. I was committed.*

Perhaps due to the emotion of the proceedings, I felt somewhat light-headed and almost toppled from my stance on the disc. Then ... just nothing, no feeling, no sensation, just nothing. I no longer had a body, just an awareness.

For a time, all around me seemed in confusion until the uncertain fog swirled and cleared. All around there seemed to be various shadows or shades which gradually resolved into figures of people. I seemed to be in the land of ghosts. I saw clearer now that the various apparitions all appeared to be dressed in their Sunday best. They wandered around speaking to one another in some soundless language; for I could hear nothing. Nor did they bother with me. It seemed that they were unable to see me. I was in another dimension and they were behind a 'glass' partition of some sort. This must be the fourth dimension that Scotus was expounding, a fourth spatial dimension.

If these were ghosts, where were all the gory visions, the gruesome images and all the traditional blood and guts? These were the images of men and women in their prime, the portrayals of how they would like to be remembered. There were men and women in

Edwardian attire mixing with Victorian ladies all in black with men sporting magnificent moustaches. There were two military men in scarlet uniforms and another three in the less glamorous khaki. Gillies in tweeds and serving girls and there was even a fiddler playing soundlessly and holding his instrument between his knees, bowing away, with some dancers quadrilling to imagined notes. There was a fair scattering of children too, one or two in sailor suits, playing hopscotch and beds with peevers, girds and cliques. A little boy in green velvet was whipping a wooden peerie side by side with a group of three girls playing with a rope, two turning and one skipping all the while chanting a silent nursery rhyme. They all ignored me. They could not see me or deigned not to see. I was of another world. I was alive and therefore could not join them. I was in a fourth spatial dimension where they were concerned - or they were the ones in the other dimension.

I remember once when walking along a Hebridean beach of white shell, I came across the wreck of an ancient rowing boat. Now its ribs stood proud of the shattered stem post and pointed skywards, a sorry sight. That is not how I remember the craft. Rather, I see it sailing through chuckling waves and proudly breasting her way to some unknown harbour. I see the vessel in its prime. So too with these shadows of bygone days, they wished to be remembered in their prime.

Little by little the figures grew fainter, more distant and I could sense the return of the fog I experienced earlier. Suddenly I was atop the grey disc and slid on its slope to the wooden floor.

I debated with myself what to do next. This was quite a discovery and the World should know of it. But should they? On the other hand, those people, those figures deserved to be left in peace not gawped at like some sideshow. They had served their time in our dimensions, surely they deserved their privacy now. My mind was made up. Somehow or other I must destroy the grey disc, the 'pewter' dish. My first instinct was to bury the curséd item. No! The answer was obvious. Loch Ness was just a couple of miles away and its sides shelved steeply to a great depth.

With much struggle and puffing and blowing, I manoeuvred the disc onto its edge and rolled it to my estate car. After further struggles, I managed to place the item in the boot lowering the back seats to extend the space. The car sagged to the limit of its suspension which hadn't happened since that time with my Auntie Jessie. I chucked the jug in to complete my load and collected my cleaning bits and pieces.

I locked up the house and made my way to the caretaker's cottage with the key. "You've had a busy time up at the big Hoose, then? Get your things OK," MacFarlane asked?

I nodded and then an idea came into my head. "You'll remember Aberlenie when it was occupied by the gentry?"

"No, no!" he replied. "That was before my time. But my father remembered those days. It was before the war, in the 1930s. The place was empty for a long time before the pop group arrived ... and they didn't stay long. Originally I think it belonged to the MacKenzies, but I can't be sure." That added up, for that was the name in the game books that you purchased at the auction.

I thanked him for his help and travelled east skirting the loch, but not really near enough to dispose of my load. Eventually I found a suitable layby near the water's edge and eased the disc from the boot of my car. I started to roll the grey dish on its edge down the slope towards the loch edge but gravity took control and it rolled faster and faster towards the Ness leaving a gouge mark in the softer ground. It entered the water and fell flat with a splash before surfing to deeper water where it sank with a sigh. I thought I could detect just a whiff of mist and then it was gone. I just hope Nessie doesn't mind.

"So you see Kenny; I seem to have achieved my lifetime ambition, some meaning to all those ancient writings and speculations and riddles. Michael Scotus had worked it out all those centuries ago."

With that he left me pondering over this, wondering over his tale, indeed over his state of mind.

Some weeks later after a long silence, I had a brief note from Dave. He was in a private hospital in some distant location on the Ayrshire coast. In the note he urged me to visit him soon. I did ponder on the urgency, yet the mention of hospital did cause concern.

Two days later, I motored down the coast to the hospital address and there he was, confined to bed and looking ghostly pale; a shadow of his former robust self. The beard somehow seemed out of place and I found it difficult to relate to the Laird of *Geal na Creag*. "Good to see you, laddie!"

Seeing my shock, he went on. "I've been here for the past six weeks, Kenny. Apparently my red cell blood count is very low and all my joints ache. I've got burn blisters on my fingers and a bit on my feet. The experts say that I have been exposed to radiation but they don't know when or how. I even had someone from Special Branch asking questions which I couldn't (or wouldn't) answer. I think we both know, though."

He picked up a laptop from his bedside table. "I never thought I would ever use one of these," he exclaimed. "I've gone all technical," he continued proudly.

I nodded in acknowledgement, still shocked.

"I've used it to find out all about Michael Scot and his connection to the Eildon hills. Sure enough, there were three hills although legend has it that Eildon started as one and the three hills were the work of Scotus. Not just that, there is a higher than normal radioactivity level in the area. They put that down to the Chernobyl Disaster . . . but we know better, don't we! We know that Michael Scotus created the first nuclear explosion in the hollow hill of Eildon."

I left David Stanford after some further chatting about this and that. On leaving, I got the impression that it was a very fulfilled David Stanford.

Some weeks later, I learned that he had gone to join his friends at Aberlenie House, I suspect.

Twixt

He opened his eyes but all around was a spinning cloud of grey. Jolly Rowbottom screwed his eyes tightly shut to wipe out the confusion of the scene without being able to eliminate the confusion from his own mind. All the time, there was a rushing sound in his ears together with a high pitched hum, for all the world like a million telegraph wires decussated by a gusting gale; for the hum rose and fell with no regular pattern. Suddenly, the whooshing and the hum change to a hollow rumble like a train entering a tunnel. Perhaps he was aboard a train ... where was he anyway?

Without him really noticing, the rumbling disappeared in a long drawn-out diminuendo until there was only the merest whisper of sound lapping at the shores of his brain. Jolly tentatively opened his eyes. The mists were clearing. He was sitting in a drab office, all buffs and browns, ochres and khakis, puces and rusts; some government department, no doubt.

"Must've been something I ate," he reflected. "Now, what had I for me dinner? For the life of me, I can't remember. Must watch what I eat! These giddy spells are getting more frequent. Must be me ticker trouble back again. Huh! And they said that the operation would finish all that . . . a bunch of quacks!"

He sat and fumed with his inner thoughts, his hands clasped over his great paunch and tried to remember why he had come to this office.

A half-frosted door opened and an elderly civil servant shuffled in to perch himself on a stool, a very hard stool, behind a tall, it seemed a very tall, desk. The papers in his claw he placed carefully and neatly at one corner of the desk.

This little bird of a man opened a large ledger and flicked quickly through the pages to stop at one. Adjusting his glasses, he crouched into the very bowels of the large book so that all that Jolly could see was a bald yellow-ochre pate surrounded by a fringe of brand-X-white hair looking like a not-so-bright halo which had fallen over the little man's ears.

Occasionally, even regularly, the bird-man would pop his head up and over the edge of his glasses to stare at Jolly Rowbottom.

Jolly in his turn studied the civil servant in an effort to get a clue as to the government department. "Wait a minute though. Maybe this was an agent's office. Maybe I decided to get a new theatrical agent after all. Certainly that last Leeds engagement was a bit of a comedown for a man of my talent. Besides, it's not so long since my Palladium days . . . doesn't look like an agent though . . . wish he'd keep still, the old parrot face."

Truly, the old man seemed to be more agitated; for his bobbing increased in frequency until, with a great show of exasperation, he slammed the ledger shut, planted his elbows on it and rested his chin in his hands. Peering over his glasses at Jolly, he almost managed a wry smile, the corners of his zip-fastener mouth just drooping perceptibly.

"Nope! I can't find you anywhere;" the old man spoke slowly and mournfully but very precisely, his chin stationary on his hands and the rest of his head moving up and down. "What is your name again?"

Again? Had he already given his name? Jolly mentally shrugged his shoulders. "J. Rowbottom . . . comedian . . . unemployed. The J. is for Jolly. Haven't you heard of Jolly Rowbottom?" Jolly stood up and planting his feet flat and wide apart; "Jolly's me name . . . jolly's me nature," he cried in his jolliest and best carrying stage voice . . . not exactly a stage whisper.

The old man winced before the blast and reopened the large ledger at the appropriate page.

". . . children's parties, garden fêtes . . ." Jolly ended weakly. "Is me name not there then?" The heavy man leaned over the large book trying to read the inverted entries.

"Can't find you, Rowbottom. Can't find you at all." The old man shook his head in despair.

He suddenly glared at Jolly as though he had just thought of something unclean. "You have come to the right place?" he asked. He grabbed the comedian's left coat sleeve to examine a large label. "Yes, ah yes, yes, yes. Your stamps are complete. Yes!"

It was Rowbottom's turn to stare. Where had the label come from? . . . or the stamps? Where was he anyway?

"Er, where is this, Mr . . . er?"

"Twixt," the old man supplied.

" . . . Mr Twixt . . ."

"No! No! That's where you are . . .Twixt . . . my little joke, you see." This time the zip fastener twitched upwards at the corners.

Jolly did not see the joke. He laughed all the same; after all people laughed at his jokes . . . some people did.

"It's funny how often I'm asked that very question; yes funny." The old man giggled to himself, pulled a handkerchief from his sleeve and blew his nose loudly. With an effort, he pulled himself together and returned to his business with Jolly Rowbottom.

"You do have an appointment for today?" His bird-like eyes held Rowbottom with their sharpness and after a little, a touch of cunning as he asked, "You wouldn't be early, rather too early, for your appointment?" Then relaxing, "No, no of course not. You don't have that look of apprehension that early arrivals have, that look of the suicide, that deep despair."

Jolly felt alarmed at this turn in the conversation. Where was he? Had he come to a headshrinker on his own volition or was it all one big mistake? What was all this talk about suicides?

"Perhaps I've come to the wrong place. I don't know no place called Twixt."

"No, no, no," the old man insisted. "This is the correct centre all right. It says so on your label. Besides, I deal with all the English ones, you know," he added proudly. "Now, let me see, let me see," he continued pulling his lower lip several times between his thumb and forefinger. "Your name is . . . em . . . Jolly Rowbottom . . . profession . . . er . . ."

"Comedian," interrupted Jolly. "You know . . . I say, I say, I say. My wife has a French lawn mower. Your wife has a French lawn mower? Yes, yes, yes. She calls it her *coup de grâce."* Jolly threw his head back and roared with laughter – very likely the reason for his singular lack of success during his stage career. Nor was he any more successful in that office, for the little man could only force an apologetic little smile which died before it was born and muttered under his breath, "I don't wish to know that!"

The civil servant made a decision. "I'll ring up records. They'll sort it out for me. We are completely modernised now, you see, computer and all. Let me see now."

He dialled two digits and waited. "Hello, hello! That you, Pete? George here. I wonder whether you can trace one of mine . . . yes, yes . . . by the name of Jolly Rowbottom . . . yes, that's his proper name . . . er, comedian, he says . . . " He paused with his hand over the mouthpiece. "He's punching a card now . . . wont be long."

He pursed his lips and rattled his pen against his fingers as he stared into the distance – twelve feet away. "Yes, Yes!" A voice was speaking at the other end again. The old man's eyebrows rose and fell and rose and fell and met; he finished with a frown. "I see. Well, I don't really see . . . Mmm . . . Most unusual! Most!"

He slowly and gently replaced the receiver onto its cradle and frowned a perplexed frown. He suddenly seemed to notice Jolly watching him. "You are late, Rowbottom, eighteen months late. Your appointment was for 16th March last year. It's now October, Rowbottom."

Jolly shook his head in bewilderment. "Eighteen months late? I can't explain it. I just can't explain it. Me appointment for the 16th March – last year?" He shook his head again. At the same instant, a look of realisation crossed his face. "Of course . . . of course! I have it!" he cried. "The 16th of March, you say? That was the week after my operation; so I wouldn't be able to keep the appointment, being in hospital, like, and then later, I probably forgot about it."

He looked at Old George eagerly but the other despairingly shook his head two or three times. "I think not," Jolly heard him mutter. "No-one forgets!" It sounded almost sinister and sent a little shiver through Jolly's whole being. Seeing his reaction, the old man tried to humour him. "Your operation was a serious one, then? You are alright now?" for he sensed that Jolly would love romancing on his medical history.

Jolly took the bait. "Serious? I'll say! Thought I was going to die. Would have done too. I still get me dizzy turns though . . . had one a little while back."

Jolly paused and drew himself up importantly. "I expect you read about it in the papers . . . it was in them all . . . quite a to-do they had about it at the time. The best piece of publicity I ever had. It was one of the first heart transplants in this . . . "

"Heart transplant?" George interrupted excitedly. "That's it, of course. I remember now. And so, you are eighteen months late . . . most inconvenient." Mumbling and grumbling, he opened a drawer in his desk and searched through a pile of paper. " Most irregular . . . "

At last, with the delight of a civil servant, he produced an enormous form from the papers and flourished it above his head. "I have it here!" he exclaimed and expertly scanned the lists and columns in the questionnaire. "Mmm. This will take me some time. A comedian did you say?"

In exasperation, Jolly turned his eyes to the ceiling. He nodded his head wearily although he now wondered who the comedian really was.

"Well, you'll have to wait until I sort this one out. "Pop in there," he nodded towards a door marked S, "and see if you can cheer up that lot. It is our waiting room for suicides."

Jolly rose and slowly walked to the door. A germ of an idea grew in his head and flourished and matured. Before he turned that handle, he knew with a tingle of exhilaration where he was.

Jolly Rowbottom opened the door and gazed at the row of chalk-white faces turned expectantly, at the same time with apprehension, towards him. "I'm here to entertain you while you're waiting, folks," he began in a breezy but rather uncertain manner . . . no response.

Jolly cleared his throat. "A very funny thing happened to me on my way . . . er . . . twixt Earth and Heaven . . . "

The Minch

Are you familiar with the Minch? It's that stretch of sea between the north Scottish mainland and the northern part of the Hebrides, Harris and Lewis and the like. Its continuation to the south separates Skye from the southern Hebrides, Benbecula and the Uists, whereas south of that there is The Sea of the Hebrides.

I don't know where the name originated but there have been suggestions that it has a French connection (*La Manche*: the English Channel) for it started appearing on maps around 1745, the date of the '45 rebellion and the association with Bonnie Prince Charlie who had serious French connections. Whatever, the seaway is associated with my narrative.

The island of Skye separates the Minch to the north from the Little Minch further south. It is guarded all round by shy little islands hiding behind each other. There are the Crowlin Isles and Scalpay and Raasay to the east. To the Southwest are the Small Islands – Eigg, Muck, Rum and Canna – all with their own beauty and legend, often mysterious and black stories. Who would guess such tales when they view the blues, the greens, the russets - but mainly the blues; for if anything the blues dominate. The prevailing legend in these parts concerns the blues, the Blue Men of the Minch and my tale concerns them.

I have a long acquaintance with the Minch. I have sailed those waters in calm and in storm, and they do say that the sea conditions are controlled by the Blue Men; when it is fine, they float dozing on the surface of the waters but when disturbed great storms erupt as they lash their tails around. The strange thing is they are only encountered in the Minch and nowhere else, or so they say.

My sailing at that time was confined to a little motor launch cruising around Loch Harport catching the odd fish and sometimes venturing into Loch Bracadale for I had then retired to Carbost on the island of Skye. This is a sleepy little place of a few houses, one or two shops and a pub – and, of course the Talisker whiskey distillery. When the car traffic dies down of an evening, the breeze is perfumed with the salt of the sea, the heather, the peat smoke and of course the Angels' Share. It is a peaceful retirement with the main (and only) town, Portree, only a short distance away, or so it seems until you realise that the Black Cuillins block the way.

It was in The Old Inn that I first met old Sandy McSween and stood him a glass of the local brew. We got talking about boats and things of the sea. It happened that he kept a small work-boat on the loch. Although the village was not geared for landing fish, he did set a few creels in the shallower parts of the bay and sold any lobsters on to the local hotels.

After a bit, we would make a point of seeking each other out to turn over the local gossip and other things, mainly the other things. The lobsters had recently been somewhat fickle and business was not that good for Sandy; his takings hardly covered the fuel costs. He was having to go further afield to lay his pots, sometimes into Loch Bracadale itself.

Late in the season, however, he struck it rich and was lifting more lobsters than he could sell. When I asked him his secret, he would just smile coyly and sip his drink. He would say no more although he did offer me one for myself on one occasion.

In winter, the westerlies would whistle round the chimneys and threatening the roofs. The sough would pull the blue peat smoke up the lum and cause the sods to glow brightly. You would think that a body would be happy to huddle round the comfort of the ingle with a good book; but not a bit of it. A person like myself enjoyed the company of others and to this end, I would brave the elements and stagger against the gale to the local hostelry. So, down the steps of the Old Inn.

On one such night, I was perched on one of the tractor seats at the bar supping a little malt when my friend, Sandy, settled next to me. For a time we talked boats and other things nautical. The various small craft had been beached for the winter and when the weather allowed, we would get on with the task of winter maintenance.

"The Blue Men are after being restless tonight," Sandy declared.

I looked at him quizzically and teasingly suggested, "I didn't think the Blue Men came this far south. They more or less stick to the Minch and round about the Shiants, don't they?"

"Not a bit of it. They would be after coming down here, if they fancied it." And left it at that.

Later we moved to a table in the corner and continued our socialising there. "You know, Kenny, I've met the Blue Men and that was in Bracadale Loch; so that's well away from their usual haunts." He hesitated, almost embarrassed.

I felt uneasy myself; for my first impulse was to laugh but I did manage to control my feelings to an indulgent smile. "And you spoke to them? I mean; did you really speak to them?"

Seeing my smile, he looked away even more embarrassed. "Well, they spoke to me first – in the Gaelic, of course."

"They spoke to you first, you say?"

"Aye! It is the way of the Blue Men. They speak in rhyme in Gaelic and you have to finish off the stanza. So I finished it."

Sandy started quoting – in Gaelic, of course; the following is a rough – very rough – translation:

" 'Your craft it cuts the finest tack to the Maidens by the head

And there you'll find the choicest fishing here to trawl;'

they said.

Chan eil maighdeannan MhicLeòid a 'toirt aire dhomh …

'Macleod's Maidens lure me not with tricks and wiles so dread;

For craft I have and steer I must for yonder rocky muoll.'

I answered; and with that they disappeared back into the depths."

"And you felt compelled to answer?"

Sandy looked at me gravely. "Oh yes or they would have been taking me with them. It's a well known fact that unless you answer with a plausible couplet, you are doomed to go with them forever – doomed – forever."

I stared at Sandy incredulous that he should believe such tales. But why should he not, for there they were, the Blue Men and if they actually did exist, why not the legend of the poems.

"I came across them again, you know on another calm day around the island of Wiay in Loch Bracadale. They were floating gently with the tide and ignored me till I set the creels in Camas na Cille. A group of Blue Men swam, like a school of dolphins, undulating towards my boat then circling, Injunes around the wagons. There was no cavalry to the rescue.

" *'Hail piscator, return ye not to Carbos, let your porridge burn,*

But swim with us round fair Vulay and thence to caves below.'

To which I replied,

Is toigh leam mo bhroilleach le specks donn ...

'But I would like my porridge, browny flecks on my return,

Weel stirred on peats by Meg wi' spurtle on the bro.' "

He regaled me with further ridiculous rhymes, which I fancy he was making up on the spot. He could tell by the glazed look in my eye that perhaps his little joke had run its course. He turned, then, to other topics still of a nautical nature and his hopes for good fishing in the coming spring.

However, a chance remark of mine brought him back to the Blue Men. I happened to recall his improvement in trapping lobsters late on in the season and I did wonder why this should occur so late in the autumn.

"It was more by chance than anything; for I was motoring in Marigold" (that's the name of his work-boat) "near the Island of Wiay and there they were again, the Blue Men – about a dozen of them. Their leader, one by the name of Seonaidh, shouted out yet another couplet,

O ghruagach ...

'O hairy chiel wi' bonny craft, come dive with us to caves below

And feast on lobster day and night or Krill if you prefer.'

You can imagine that I was getting the boak by this time and my dander was up – a chiel, indeed! I was going to give them 'chiel'.

'Awa ye go an' bide in caves that honour I bestow

And eat yer sunfish spines an' aw to catch your curséd craw' "

"They turned their grey faces to me in horror and churned the sea with their tails before diving below the Marigold spinning her round. For a time, all was quiet but black clouds were gathering over the Cullins threatening a change in the weather. I turned up to full throttle and made full six knots for the shelter of Bracadale before the storm finally broke. You yourself know how quickly the Minch can change and always, you have to keep one eye into the south west. Anyway, I haven't seen the Blue Men since; in a way, I miss them and the challenge of the Gaelic poems."

"You still haven't told me of your luck with the lobsters."

"The lobsters? Oh yes, that will be the lobsters!" observed Sandy, with his mind miles away. "Well I notice my friends and tormentors always seemed to surface around the same region to the south of Wiay, you know, where all the caves are at *Geodha nan Faochad.* The Blue Men kept blethering on about all the lobsters they feast on. Well, I'll drop my creels there – and bingo – I struck gold. Day after day I was hauling in my pots, often with a catch, whiles two to a pot."

He smiled secretly. "I'm sure they can spare a few for me," and then with some agitation, "But dinna say a word to the anyone!"

We left it at that; not that I believed his outlandish nonsense about Blue Men and all that. I feel he just wanted to keep his fishing patch a secret from any prying ears – if ears can pry.

** *

The following spring arrived early and Sandy was there at the floating pier loading his creels on the little boat; indeed, so many creels that the boat seemed top heavy. I suppose he knew what he was doing.

"Hoping for another bumper season, Sandy?" And he just smiled in a sort of coy way.

"I'm just off to catch some mackerel first. Fetch your boat and we'll catch them together."

Together we motored North through a kind sea with a pod of dolphins bow-riding before they got bored and went off to charm someone else. A basking shark sauntered past waving a languid dorsal fin. I waved back. There was a yellow sunfish lazily drifting with the tide. This time I didn't wave at the bag of bones.

For a time, we fished and caught the mackerel with Sandy baiting his pots as we drifted along with the tide in Loch Bracadale. Around the middle of the day, he made for more open water and left me to my own fishing with a brief wave of his hand.

The last that I saw of him was the outline of his stocky figure against the boat's cuddy. Indeed, it was the last I saw of him at all.

I no longer have a boat; nor do I fish or sail now. I have left Carbost for a house on the mainland far from the sea – something to do with the Blue Men.

Black Art

Tom Moodie was the Firm's character. How he ever reached the higher echelons of the board I'll never know; for as far as I could see he appeared to spend his hours in the senior canteen-come-restaurant . . . that is, those hours that were licensed to sell strong liquor; for Tom was also the Firm's alcoholic. It was at the bar end of the canteen last week that we got to talking about old times, good and bad.

Now Tom was a peculiarly enigmatic mixture of the military (retd. Late of the 5th Foot or something) and the eternal show-off. The military bearing was enhanced by a toothbrush moustache over stainless steel fillings, steel blue eyes under white bushy eyebrows and the lot topped by close cut steel grey hair, all amply relieved by his sanguine complexion. The strange fact was that, although his great booming voice was seldom without a slur, I'd never actually seen Tom drunk.

As conversations go, ours was nothing remarkable. The only thing we had in common was Glasgow University so that inevitably our talk turned there.

“I was a late starter, you know,” Tom remarked. “Had no intention of going in for this science lark.”

I mumbled something like, “Oh yes?” to encourage him, but not too much.

“Yep,” and his voice lowered to a confidential level. “I was all set to carve myself a career on the stage, you know. I might have made it too had it not been . . .“ His voice trailed away and I looked up expectantly, but he was staring into the dregs of gin in the glass nestled between his pink well-manicured fingers. I ordered two more drinks and listened to his story.

** *

I had built up quite a reputation for myself as a young amateur magician so that you can imagine that this went to my head quite a bit. There was no mountain too high, no river too deep etc. etc. With stars in my eyes, there was no stopping me after hitting top of the bill at the local Scout Hall with – Moodie’s Magic.

Not that my skill was to be scoffed at, although I say it myself. Where sleight of hand was concerned, I had a master teacher in that great magician, Johnny Ramsay. He gave me my grounding in such effects as the Mysterious Cups and Balls. Then there was a whole series of thimble sleights which I later mixed with some of

Edward Proudlock's routine – oh, and lots of other bits and pieces, coins and ropes, cigarettes and billiard balls. I was soon to find, though, that the variety stage was very, very different to the local church hall.

Still, I was young; I was resilient. The trickles of applause petering out to stony silence, even ribald remarks and laughter, were hint enough that something was very wrong. Something was certainly needed to perk up my act. It was some time, however, before I found out what it was.

It was during a week's engagement at Bradford (which turned out to be a one-night stand) when the manager said to me at the end of the first house, "What thee needs lad is summit big we can all see." That was it, of course. They couldn't see what I was doing. What I needed was an illusion of two – entertainment not cleverness.

"Tom!" I said to myself. "Tom! Black art is the answer."

Black Art was an idea I had seen some years previously in an old *Sphinx* magazine and my friend, Chung Ling Soo had encouraged me in this. The idea is simple enough and had been used in vaudeville before but latterly had fallen out of favour for some reason or other. I set about constructing my equipment, for all that was required was a small stage set on the main stage. This miniature stage I completely draped in black and set a square of naked light bulbs round the proscenium. Using this device and with the aid of an assistant, I could perform all sorts of miracles; for within this stage my assistant, dressed completely in black velvet, could move around unseen. The lift of a black foulard and a table would appear … chairs floating in mid-air were child's play … ghostly chalk wrote ghostly messages … there was no end of mysteries I could perform with this device.

My next engagement at Leeds Palace of Varieties was a great success; and let me tell you, Leeds folks are the very devil to please. I presented the Black Art magic together with a few sleight of hand fillers to add to the variety. But most of the act was a matter of waving my arms about 'in mysterious fashion' and mutter a few spells and magical phrases … Gorgonzola Flibbertygibbit … another table appears covered in masses of flowers … round of applause … a bowed acknowledgement.

Then, just as we were getting into our stride – the Wednesday of the first week, it was – Dud, my assistant, gets up and goes. He said he didn't like the act because his name never appeared on the posters. Well! I mean to say! It would give the whole game away, wouldn't it? So there I was with a zinger of an act but no sheet anchor. Still, not to despair! A stage hand by the name of Nick Clootie volunteered . . . when I presses a few quid into his hand. In any case, the operation of the Black Art stage was quite simple; it was a matter of doing things carefully and in their correct order.

After a few mishaps, Nick and myself got through to the end of the week and prepared a few new settings for the following week. I can tell you straight too that it was downright slog in that hall of variety in the summer season, two houses a night, six nights a week – no rest for the wicked!

Perhaps I was a bit curt with Nick during the first house the following Monday. Oh, I know he messed things up a bit when he produced two white rabbits when it should have been a basket of fruit. All in all, he was doing alright. I can't remember now what cutting remark I delivered into the black velvet of that miniature stage. All I know is that I couldn't find Nick after the act and we still had the second house to do.

The stage manager wasn't very pleased, I can tell you. "We can't cut twenty minutes from the show. They'll pull the place apart." I could well believe it. "You'll just have to do it yourself and I'll get the band to back you. Yes! You'll just have to do it yourself. I'll just introduce you as Moodie's Ghost." What could I do?

Funnily enough, the show was a great success and we decided to carry on with the same pattern for the rest of the week.

I was too excited to notice much that first Monday night but as the week progressed it struck me that, in spite of my heavy black velvet rigout, my little stage was inordinately cold. I always did think that Leeds was a cold part of the country, but this was something different. With all the lighting on stage, it seldom is cold there ... unless you're playing to an empty theatre. Then it's very cold.

It wasn't till the manager dropped a chance remark about the act that I got to thinking. What did he mean by, "I liked the bit when the luminous skeleton appeared as Terry (he was the band's drummer) played that part on the rhythm skulls"? What skeleton? There was no skeleton in my act.

Little things led to greater. More and more, the act was taken out of my hands. Unrehearsed ghostly hands wrote ghostly smoky messages in the chill air of my little stage. All around, tables appeared and danced and jigged and tumbled about leaving me in the centre of it all in great confusion of mind till at last, I could stand it no longer. I left the jokers, whoever they were, to the seemingly joyful task of taking over my act. Jokers! Hobgoblins more like, or spooks, or some such phantasm. I'd had enough. I escaped from the rigour of that half-lighted box through a double flap in the black drape.

I stood there for, oh I don't know how long, with my teeth chattering before it got through to my dull senses that I had a bottle of the best in my dressing room. I discarded my velvet hood and groped my way along the dim corridor to the room at the end.

The room was brightly lit when I got there, a welcome relief from that chill stage, and there waiting to greet me was Nick Clootie and an old friend of mine, Chung Ling Soo. Soo seemed startled when he saw me; I suppose with the black cloak I did look like the Angel of Death, but my greeting reassured him. Even more reassurance, for I produced my bottle of whiskey from the bottom drawer of my dressing table – not any old whiskey but a fine malt Bruichladdich.

Now as you know, Soo was the one who encouraged me by getting me into the business in the first place and at the time, I was rather grateful for it. I was not so grateful to Clootie but I could now understand why he quit so readily. He must have shared my experience of that dread stage. Perhaps I should tell you too that Soo was an old friend of my father from his time in the US of A; for in spite of his Chinese name and act, he was American through and through.

"Hi there, Tom lad! That's real civilized of you," Soo said warming to the drink. "Thought ya were the devil himself," he went on casting a sly glance at Clootie.

Thereafter, the conversation drifted on mainly to the great illusions of Chung Ling Soo; for make no mistake about it he *was* one of the great illusionists of his day. Ah yes, his rice cans were to be marvelled at ... his linking rings perfection. Did you ever see him catch a bullet in his teeth? No, before your time, eh? And his Chinese parasol was a real deception. Still, mustn't get carried away.

I was carried away, though, by events on that night, I can tell you. The excitement of having my patron (so to speak) there in my dressing room had chased all sense of time from my mind, and there I was with still the second house to run. Gone was my former terror. In the panic of the moment, all I could think of was the preparation for the second house and the fact that Chung Ling Soo would be out there watching my performance.

I hurriedly excused myself and rushed down the dim corridor leading to the stage. The safety curtain was down and over in the wings on the prompt side, the stage manager was talking to one of the hands. He spotted me, waved a hand and wandered over.

"Great stuff, Tom. The show was great, just great. It'll really bring in the crowds tomorrow."

Let me tell you, I was puzzled. "Tomorrow? Why tomorrow?"

"It was the second house tonight, Tom. I've never seen anything like it. Terrific! Flashes, thunder, the lot."

The second house!

Tom Moodie sat there staring at his empty glass. He looked up and caught my eye. He smiled rather wistfully.

"Did you complete the week then, Tom?" I asked with ghoulish curiosity.

"Good Lord no!" he exclaimed. "Didn't have the nerve. You see, Chung Ling Soo was killed that very night in London performing his bullet catching illusion. He was shot."

Tom swirled an imaginary drink in his empty glass. "I did try a come-back later," he went on avoiding my eyes, "but every time I went on stage, the boards beneath me seemed to gurn and screech as though a goat were scraping his horns neath my feet."

Suddenly, he looked up, his eyes blazing, his breath fast like a desperate man. "You're the first I've told, but that damned devil down there was Nick Clootie ... Old Clootie ... Old Nick!"

** *

Yes, three today . . . Tom's funeral is at three.

Nimrod

Carl Rausen's lips tightened into a thin straight line as he nestled the butt of his Steyr Zephyr II into a more comfortable position. He settled his tanned cheek gently along the rifle stock and peered through the telescopic sights. A light breeze whispered from the pines bringing with it the fragrance of terpines mixed with the savour of bog myrtle crushed under his weight. It mingled with his body odour as it stirred the short straw hair of his head. His grey eyes narrowed and relaxed again. Yes, he had allowed for that breeze.

A slight movement in the shadow of the copse edge – shadow into sunshine resolved black into dapple brown as the doe nibbled her way into the clearing. What a beaut! Oh I know that deer shooting is out of season. Still, who's to know! This god-forsaken place is miles from anywhere. No-one, apart from an occasional forestry bod, walks this stretch between the Eglin and Gala Lanes.

The dry grass rustled as Rausen brought his rifle to bear once more. Fully a quarter of a mile away the doe, her back to the wind, raised her head , peered straight down his sights and lowered her head again. Nibble, nibble, nibble, ten yards nearer. The hunter adjusted the sights to four hundred yards. For a moment his eyes strayed from his quarry. Once more, the rifle was aligned. Rausen squinted down the telescope. The cross-wire drifted down just behind the ear . . . an awkward angle full face on . . . mental check on wind . . . take up first pressure on the trigger . . . hair trigger now . . . steady.

Crack! The rifle leaped and jolted his head back. Carl Rausen quivered through his large frame and a doe died … out of season.

Rausen stood away from the grassy bank which had been his stalking cover and lighted a cigarette. The smoke trickled from his nostrils and whipped behind him in the wind. He smiled to himself. A full four hours he had spent stalking this game, four hard and sometimes cramped hours. Now he had done it. Pity it hadn't been a stag, though; much more satisfying.

He lifted his rifle together with his knapsack and scrambled down the slope towards the trees. He could just see the dapple brown of his kill at the edge of the trees. A photograph, perhaps, and then leave the carcass to rot where it lay. Doe doesn't make good eating. In the easier walk towards the wood, Rausen removed his twin lens reflex from the knapsack and checked the setting. None of that digital stuff – this was a real camera with real film. You can do so much more with real film. Now that he was closer, the dead doe seemed so much smaller than he remembered, hardly worth recording. A quick photograph and he would be away before the shot attracted any busybody.

The doe was lying in some long rushes by a draining ditch. He prodded it with the toe of his boot and turned it over. As it rolled into the ditch, its head came into view. The open eyes stared darkly at the man through the red splatter that was once a face, a girl's face. My God, it's a girl. I've killed a girl!

Rausen stared down at the body in the ditch. It was all an accident. He didn't know it was a girl. It must have been the brown swede coat. But that long hair, how did he miss noticing her long hair in the telescopic sights. They would never believe him.

Desperately he looked round for something to put over the corpse. He would bury it. Yes, that's what he would do. A ready made grave in this ditch . . . but a filled-in ditch would be noticed. Someone is sure to try and clear it. Another hole, that's it; he must look for another hole. He scrambled over the ditch towards the pines. The soft pine-needle ground would be easy to dig, or perhaps he would find a small natural hollow all ready made.

Rausen reached the trees just as he heard the shot and the smack as the bullet bit into the tree beside him. He dropped flat and wriggled desperately behind the roots of a large pine. Another shot and the bullet entered the tree just in front of his face. Instinctively he drew back but not before splinters of bark pierced the skin over his cheekbone. He could taste the salt of his own blood. Wild-eyed, he looked round . . . must find better cover . . . where's my gun? Dammit! Back there at the ditch . . . put it down to use my camera . . . can't get it now . . . just this stupid camera.

A pine wood is no place to be caught by an adversary. Just by crouching, anyone can see for distances of a hundred yards or more in some directions; for the undergrowth is negligible and the lower three feet or so of each tree is cleared of branches by forestry workers. Rausen knew this. He also knew that, since the trees were planted in straight lines, there were also blind spots. He had no option but to hope that by following the line of trees, he could stay out of sight long enough to avoid his pursuer pulling a bead on him.

Rausen held his breath and listened motionless for half a minute, his ears twitching animal-like. This is it. It's now or never. Half bent, he crashed into the depths of the pine forest, running blindly at first, then taking care to follow the trees in a line. Needles scratched at his face, branches tugged at his sleeve, knocked at his head, pulled at his hair as though they were living things. Once, he stopped to listen and over the thumping of his heart he could hear the snapping and crashing behind him. Onward he ran till green light in front showed the edge of the forest. Bursting through into the harshness of bright sunlight, Rausen could see the dark green fingers of another forest waiting. He had merely stumbled across a firebreak.

Must get clear of this forest! Up this break should get me away from this . . . no cover amongst these trees. He scrambled over a wide ditch and followed a mean path through whins and bramble and bracken, up and along the firebreak. The going was fierce and sapped the energy of the strong man. The heat of the day's sun seemed trapped in this place together with half the flies, burrow bugs and clegs of the country. They worried his scratched face, sipped the sweat of his brow and gorged on his blood. Pausing to suck in great rasping lungfuls of air, he imagined he could hear downhill, the snapping of twigs . . . or was it the sighing of the wind rubbing the trees together. Must get on! Must get out of this hell-fire.

The firebreak gradually twisted round and climbed the side of the hill till Rausen felt the heat of the sun on the back of his tired head.

This must be the west side of Craigmawhannel. If only he could rise above the tree line he could find a landmark to guide him from this mess. The path was clearer as the bracken and overgrowth thinned. The break widened into a V as the two forests spread away to the north and south. At long last he was clear; he would be able to see Loch Doon and safety.

The desperately panting man threw himself over the wire boundary fence and into the short heather beyond. He rolled over behind a convenient stone where he lay in its shadow, face down dragging the perfume laden air into his lungs. Rausen trembled violently with emotion as he considered his position. He had killed some unknown, interfering female who aught not to have been there in the first place. Not only that, someone had seen him; someone who felt deeply enough to kill him. Didn't he realise it had been an accident? Or was it an accident? Had he been so blindly intent on killing that he had failed identified his quarry? The madness of the whole situation brought a certain calm to Burt Rausen. He must keep his head and think his way out of this place and situation. After all, he was an expert hunter. He could stalk the most difficult of animals – so why not man - this man who was pursuing him?

Burt raised himself and peered carefully round the edge of the boulder. Dust from the trees had settled on his face and dried the blood on his cheek into a long black streak. There below, the silver fronds of waving pines glistened in the sunlight but revealed nothing. All his senses were alert, as indeed they had to be when stalking. His eyes and ears detected nothing, but his twitching nose identified an animal smell, the stench of his own fear. Smack and a whine – the bullet ricocheted from a spot above his head and showered him with grey lichen.

For an endless moment, Rausen froze against the face of the boulder before his faculties returned. A quick squirm through the short heather and he was into the lee of the rock. There, not a hundred yards off, was a dry stone dyke . . . must make it . . . a quick dash and a leap over the top . . . but not before another bullet spattered into the wall haven.

Rausen lost no time. Under cover of the dyke he raced uphill. Just once he stopped to catch his breath and risked a careful glance over the wall in the direction of the now-distant woodland. No pursuer had yet emerged. He frowned. Was the stalker playing with him? At no time during the pursuit had he seen his adversary . . . most perplexing. Was it the ghost of the girl in brown chasing him? He laughed bitterly at his stupid little joke.

The wall led Rausen round the side of Hooden's Hill on to the bare rock-strewn slopes of Yellow Tomach. So far so good! No sight nor sound of whoever it was.

Rausen paused in a short gulley between two protecting slabs of stone. His thoughts had calmed to an even logical Teutonic level. What would he do in the other's situation? It was a pretty safe guess that Rausen would keep in the protection of that dyke as long as he could. From the dyke, the obviously easiest route was that very path he was following to the peak of Mulwharcher. Instead, if he somehow managed to drop unseen into the valley, he had a fair chance of making good time to Loch Doon – and safety.

Down towards Gala Lane, Rausen could see the inviting lush green of the valley floor. That would be his objective. Dropping over a short rock-fall, he followed the ledge down the side of the mountain. How open and exposed it was on the ledge! Rausen shivered at the thought. There was nothing above him, no sign of his adversary, and as long as the ledge curved to the right, no one could take a long shot at him. The convex face of the rock would protect him and even though he was moving south away from Loch Doon, at least this route would take him to the valley below.

The ledge terminated. It stopped abruptly at a scree fall which rattled gently and slithered downward as he watched it. He could scramble across those ever moving plates of stone for he noticed that a continuation of the ledge curved off to the left. The prospect of such exposure was not pleasant. There was only one choice; down the scree-fall.

Rausen felt the insecurity, quicksand-like, the almost living ground beneath him as he stepped on to the slate. Facing downhill, he kneaded the loose schist with his feet as he gathered momentum down that critical angle of rock. By making the motions of walking backwards, he managed to manoeuvre his route past the larger outcrops of rock till at last the large and badly bruised man careened into the larger rocks at the bottom of the scree. A small avalanche of slate rattled round the ankles of the panting man. Before him the level too, too green valley stretched to the river and beyond.

With a thrill of horror, Rausen gazed at the endless expanse of green. He seemed hypnotised by what? Its beauty? Hardly - He was in no mood for such thoughts – Could he really believe his eyes? No, it couldn't be! A late rock from the avalanche confirmed his worst fears. It outran the edge of the debris and plopped into the green. An ever widening shockwave of ripples ran over the verdant morass to lose itself in a sphagnum infinity. The whole valley bottom was a floating watery moss. The Gala Lane had burst its banks.

In desperation, Rausen hunted around for another escape route. The rubble of the rock fall would be difficult . . . must hurry . . . must get out of here. Another rattle of stones from the scree startled him into looking up. There, not a hundred yards away, was the man with the rifle . . . my rifle! His approach was rapid so that in no time the two men, the hunter and the hunted were within spitting distance. Can't get away ... point blank range. Quite illogically, Rausen raised his camera and shot; but what could mere film do! A flood of red overwhelmed him . . . no shot . . . no pain . . . just spinning and falling . . . nothing.

***

"Yes, Inspector. Jaikie Kennedy the ranger, noticed him in the Tauchers from the shoulder of the hill there. He noticed the hoodies too".

"The hoodies?" the inspector queried.

"Yes, the crows," the sergeant continued. "It could have been a fall from the rock up there. It's pretty rotten slatey stuff."

The inspector examined the body carefully, almost distastefully. He straightened and turned to the victim's belongings . . . not a lot of help there. "The man's in remarkably good shape, apart from his head. Do you think he fell, sergeant? Or was someone after him?"

The sergeant nodded sagely although he didn't really think. He wasn't paid to think. "I sent the film for developing, sir," the sergeant ventured.

"Film? What film? Oh, from this camera; of course, it's not a digital one. The camera's a bit battered, don't you think? Pity; it looks like a classic." The inspector prodded it with his foot just as the developed film arrived.

"What do you think of this last print, sir?"

The inspector looked at the photograph. "Magnificent! It really is a magnificent shot. A twelve point stag, I'd say; and the way it's throwing its head against that sky . . . truly magnificent!"

Me Down There

A few droplets of water stood proud of the polished oak surface like dull glass beads on a cheap jewel box. Even the brass plaque bearing the legend 'James Dunlop Spearman, R.I.P.' lacked any gleam of life and had started to tarnish in the November damp. It was as though the heavens had said, "Let's at least grieve a little for the corpse" and sent as a token a mere skittering of rain. Looking down into that open grave, I paid my last respects, such as they were, to an empty body, such as it was.

Raising my eyes from the settled coffin, I looked around at the solemn clad, grim faced figures and wondered just what they understood (or guessed) about the whole affair. Perhaps if they knew what *I* knew, they would no longer wonder why I, an eminent surgeon by name William Lavery, should have known this man. Certainly we were in the same age group along with a million or so others in the country, so that possibly we were friends. Yes, that was it; paying his last respects to an old friend. But James Spearman had no friends, only money.

So these were his nearest and dearest so to speak, his only relatives come for the big share out. Little did they know the conditions of the will. I did. As I said, I was in on the whole affair from the beginning right from the time that Spearman consulted me in London, initially as an 'old friend'. Oh yes, I was an old friend . . . the clinical tests . . . the drawing up of the special terms of the will . I was even in at the kill, to coin a phrase.

My gaze followed the mourners as they slowly broke away from the graveside in discrete little groups, almost huddled together so that you could imagine them whispering - about what? Ha! Back to the will again! Only a young man tended by a nurse remained. His invalid chair sank into the wet clay as the nurse struggled to push him nearer till eventually he decided that that was close enough. He could see into the full length of the grave. The young man, his eyes so black, almost feverish in contrast to his pale parchment face, stared at the coffin until a breeze from nowhere sprinkled his face with raindrops from a nearby naked poplar and stirred him from his trance. He looked up directly at me as though he knew I had been watching him. His mouth twisted into a crooked grin unexpectedly and he seemed to wink. I had a fleeting impression he was laughing.

An imperious signal to his nurse and they turned around and on to the hard gravel path once more. I fell into step alongside the wheeled man and spoke to him. "I see that you're recovering well from your accident. You were most determined to come to the funeral."

He smiled his crooked smile again and fingered a large plaster on the side of his head as he continued to stare straight in front. "Marvellous funeral, marvellous!" he said in a slurred manner like a Friday night drunk, over and over again. Slowly he turned to me. "Did you see my sister Jane? She put on a marvellous show, don't you think? Marvellous! Sniffing into that hanky and thinking of all that lolly." He sniggered and caught a few disapproving glances from the group just ahead.

"I say, Lavery," he whispered. "Did you do as I suggested? Stand upwind to avoid the mothballs." And he chuckled again much to my embarrassment.

I dismissed the nurse for the moment and took over pushing the invalid chair for the next few yards in an angry silence from me and an occasional stifled snort from him.

"I say, Lavery," he burbled at last; "I say, what would they think if they knew it was me down there?"

***

Many years later after I had retired to my place in Bermuda, I got round to telling this strange tale to a close friend of mine.

However, I felt that I had to elaborate somewhat as I could see that the friend was all agog to know why the young man had reacted in such a way and why he was making such curious statements; so I continued the tale.

The young man's name was Norman Spearman Watt, a distant relative by his way of it; hence the Spearman. If the truth be known though, he was no relative at all, that is to say, not a blood relative. Well not really. It is all so difficult to explain without telling you the whole story. Indeed, I do not see why I should not tell you now that it is done and gone these twenty or more years.

About twenty years ago, or was it yesterday, James Spearman first visited me in my consulting rooms. I was in Westmorland Street just off Harley Street at that time and was building quite a reputation for myself as a consultant and practising surgeon. In his case, it took only a few clinical tests and X-rays to confirm that Spearman was desperately ill. A particularly virulent form of stomach cancer was so advanced that I classed him, without much hesitation, as a terminal case. There was little I could do but recommend a nursing home where he could spend his last few days under sedation. His vast fortune, which he had accumulated in a mere fifteen years, was of little avail now. Besides he had come to the wrong man. I was a neurologist with a particular interest in computers and I told him as much.

"No! You're the man for the job alright, Lavery," he stated in his own blunt way "and I'm prepared to pay, and pay well, for a special, a very special job of work."

At my puzzled silence, he continued, "I've followed your research very carefully and that last paper particularly on computer linked signals from nerve networks. Fascinating stuff! Made my fortune flogging computers so I understand what you're getting at."

A spasm of pain arrested his flow for an instant and distracted him long enough for me to start up my hidden recorder. I find that my memory can be faulty sometimes when I want to recall exact statements from my patients; so often analyses of these statements proves valuable when assessing their condition; unethical perhaps, but very useful. Besides no one need know.

Spearman rallied sufficiently to resume; "From what you've told me, Lavery, there's no hope left, is there! Cash or no cash, I've just about had it."

I murmured some platitude about there always being hope but he abruptly waved it aside with a dismissive gesture. He paused. "I want to be the first," he blurted out and again seeing my puzzlement continued, "I know sufficient about your work to see just where you're going. I can see your ultimate aim and I want to be the first."

I must admit I hedged at first. I too knew where I was going but was not yet ready to reveal this to the medical profession far less a layman, particularly a layman like Spearman. "Look here, Lavery; what do you do in that nursing home of yours? You have facilities there for a job like this surely?" and for the first time he seemed to hesitate; for he could see that he had hit the nail on the head. I just did *not* have the equipment for the job, as he called it.

We were short of a special type of computer with 3-D imaging and here he was sitting in my consulting room answering my computer prayer. "I'll have it there tomorrow," he promised. "Now will you do the job?"

I mumbled something about tissue rejection but he was for none of that. "That's fixed then, Lavery. I arrive at your nursing home tomorrow complete with computer and a couple of programmers. You can start preparing me for the special day. I'll leave the procurement of a suitable body up to you. You'll have better contacts than me in that line."

"That's it then! The first brain transplant in history," and he chuckled away to himself; "Or rather, the first body transplant!" He returned to his chuckling until a stab of pain reminded him what it was all about.

Obtaining a suitable body was much simpler than I had imagined. It was a young man of about twenty three whose brain was sorely damaged by a malignant tumour. It had reached such a state that the higher faculties of speech and sight had gone and even the impulse to his heart had ceased so that he was being kept alive solely on machines - truly a cabbage, a medical curiosity. Blood grouping matched Spearman's so that as near an ideal situation as I could have hoped for presented itself. A quiet word with McFarlane of the Eastern General and with the near relatives of the young man fixed things remarkably quickly and, need I say it, to the cash satisfaction of all concerned!

The transplant itself, although complex, was clear in my own mind and I mapped the procedure on paper before committing the plan to the computer programmers. My main worry was the after effects and the probability of tissue rejection.

Preparing the donor body was simple enough; for it was already being kept alive on machines - pacemaker - artificial lung - kidney machine - drip feed into a hand. The old damaged brain was removed and the exposed nerve ends were washed with an isotonic solution of my own formulation. This solution removed the membrane from the nerve tissue in preparation for its subsequent treatment.

James Dunlop Spearman; I absolve all concerned from all blame in the event of an unsuccessful operation; a final technicality.

Spearman's brain was removed from his cranium in one complete unit of course to the background chug chug chugging of the peristaltic pumps. Our little team of five watched fascinated as the large grey-pink pulsating walnut seemed to shiver slightly under the fluorescent lighting and the uncertain optical conditions created by the saline spray. The brain itself was supported on a fluidized bed as gentle and soothing as any goose down.

Side by side, the body and brain were ready for fusion into one being. By increasing the fluid flow through the bed, the brain was raised and manoeuvred into its new foundations of delicate meninges membranes. One by one the main blood vessels, arteries and veins were married to complete the first main step. The brain was now a part of its new body using its blood and replenishing its cells. A massive dose of the anti-rejection drug made sure of that. Now to the matching of the nerve tissue.

Up till that time, the big problem in performing a brain transplant was in the matching of the nerve tissue of the brain with that of the body. One crossed line, so to speak, meant that a signal which was conditioned to twitch an eyebrow might instead kick someone in the pants. There was no method for identifying the functions of the various nerves simply from their bared ends. Now I had the answer to all that. My high-state computer attached to the various banks of nerves could select each end in turn and identify it from the type and magnitude of its signal impulse. The size of the impulse characterised the nerve's general function; the waveform and decay curve specified more exactly its correlation. Similarly the nerves from the rest of the body were identified. The computer even completed the process by 'welding' together the nerve ends using benzoyl peroxide to stimulate the polymerisation process - a sort of plastic joint.

Starting with the *medulla oblongata* the automatic brain functions were restored one by one - breathing - heart beat - the gastric juices - nerve after nerve after nerve. This middle section of the brain lasted about five hours with the computer doing all the work. Then all we could do was wait and watch. Any resultant sign, any twitch would be a result. The next twenty hours were spent waiting in two-hour shifts with us doing all the twitching.

Resting in an adjoining room, I waited unable to sleep and thinking of the foolhardy way I had taken up Spearman's challenge before I was really ready. Then I thought, should this be successful, this first brain transplant, I was made. On the other hand, should everything go bottom up - must thrust such thoughts from my mind - after all, I still have a new state-of-the-art computer; and no one need be any the wiser.

Alarm bells! Something had happened.

"I saw it Bill, I saw it." Doc MacFarlane was dancing round the surgery. "His larynx moved, Bill. It moved."

I sighed with relief. Something was working. "2 units of adrenaline, Sandy, and we'll see what develops. That should kick-start his heart."

In the days following things progressed at an astonishing rate and within the month, Spearman was up and walking a few paces. For convenience sake, he was now calling himself Norman Spearman Watt; it seemed appropriate that he include Spearman in his new name. Little did I know the real purpose.

The material problems were apparent, or so I thought. Firstly, I had one frozen body (minus brain) to dispose of; secondly, Spearman Watt had no cash to cover the considerable costs of the whole process. In addition, I couldn't really announce my success to the world. I didn't know the legal situation regarding the operation. I had to have it out with the patient.

I called at his room in the nursing home and placed myself on one of the upright chairs laying my papers on a low coffee table. I think he knew what I had on my mind. He leaned back at ease in his soft chair and looked quite smug at my unease.

"Now look here Spearman, or rather, Spearman Watt. I'm really in a difficult situation, you know."

He grinned. "I know. I've worked it all out though." He went on to detail what he thought we should do to resolve the situation.

"What! You want me to defrost your old body and present it as though you had only recently died?"

He grinned again. "You see, before we started all this I drew up my latest Last Will and I left everything to Norman Spearman Watt; yes, everything to me!"

"But your relatives ... they're sure to contest it for there's no such person ... "

"Ah! I thought of that too. You see, I pinched this identity from some church burial records. So all you have to do is provide the body and a death certificate. Get a relative in to identify the body and we're home and dry."

"What if the relatives refuse? In view of the will, they might."

"They are not aware of the latest version. All they know, with all their prying, is that they all stand to gain, considerably! They know nothing of this new version or of the 'long lost cousin'."

He was still amused at the prospect of witnessing his greedy, grasping relatives at the reading of the will. As a beneficiary he would, of course be there as the mysterious cousin.

Afterwards, he told me with some glee all about the occasion. Who was this stranger they had never even heard of, this upstart? Their reaction was almost predictable and yes, they would contest the will. That meant that the assets would be tied up until the whole affair was settled. That left Spearman-Watt with a bit of an embarrassing situation; for he had no funds to speak of.

"Look, Lavery. I want you to bankroll me till the whole thing is settled."

He saw me hesitate for more than a moment. "I don't think you have much option, comrade. I've been thinking about the whole process of the operation and the disposal of my body and the various other irregularities."

So began the blackmail process. I had been looking forward to announcing my successful operation process to the world but I could see the difficult situation he had manoeuvred me into and there was no way I could present my work as a *fait accompli.* Oh yes, I could still write learned papers on the possibilities of my techniques in brain transplant, but it would not be accepted until it had been tried in practice. From that day forth, I was trapped into being his piggy bank. Not only that; he changed his supervising doctor just in case I was tempted to arrange any 'unfortunate' change to his state of health.

***

Lavery stared for a time at the blue waters of the Caribbean sparkling with sun-reflexions and sipped his pina colada. His companion waited expectantly but could wait no longer. "So what happened? Did he blackmail you or what?"

Lavery still hesitated. Finally, "Oh, it was all resolved eventually. The patient died."

Silence.

"Yes, the operation was not really a success. I was rushed into the whole affair and had not fully researched the background, well, not as thoroughly as I should have."

He paused before continuing; "It was the nerve polymerisation process. The problem was the benzoyl peroxide. You see, it was an addition polymerisation involving free radicals; and free radicals are a recognised source of cancer. Not long after the operation, he developed a cancerous tumour at the top of his spine which, although painful, he daren't let his doctor know for it would expose his full medical history including the brain operation. Then the whole affair would come out and destroy his contested-will case."

"It got a brief mention in the papers. He died and the grasping relatives inherited. I got a computer."

O'Malley's Store

Do you remember the last war? Hitler's war. No! Of course you won't ... before your time. Things were rationed then, food and other stuff. It was pretty bad here in the North East for the main food centres were near the west coast ports or London. Any little that was going, we were the last to hear about it ... always last in the queue.

I was in Admiralty research at that time ... salt water corrosion in boiler condensers, if I remember rightly ... so that I was doing quite a bit of travelling up and down the country mostly between Birkenhead and Clydebank and occasionally over here. Just as well too, for the family were living here in the North East and any and every occasion I could, I would pick up some little food item on my travels.

I remember stopping off overnight in Carlisle on one of these journeys; it would be near the beginning of the war, probably early 1940. I put up in Charlie Dank's place, the Bell and Crown. I usually did when I was in the area since it was so handy for the station, near the castle, if you know Carlisle ... quite small but a comfortable clean little place. Anyway, as I was saying, I was signing into the place for the night when this tall bean-pole of a man staggered through the swing doors of the hotel.

Drunk, did you say? Well, not exactly although I suspect that he maybe had a wee bit something inside to help him along, so to speak. No! He was staggering under the weight of a side of bacon. Without a word, he drew the hotel register towards him and signed his name. Equally unmoved, Charlie lifted the key to room 22 and handed it to him.

"You'll not be taking that upstairs, sir," Charlie said in his gruffest tone.

The other turned slowly and said in a thick Irish brogue, "I will be takin' it up and I am takin' it up, so there. It's been with me all the way from Ireland and we'll not be parted now." His eyes were beady, almost hooded, the veins in his face purple and broken and his sparse grey moustache drooped over a drooping mouth. His face grew little.

At that point, the Irishman's taxi driver entered struggling under the weight of a large sack of something ... could it be sugar ... and leant against the reception desk.

"Room 22," the Irishman said, "and oi'll make it worth your while."

The two men staggered up the stairway with their loads. Charlie? He just threw up his hands in despair; for he was really a softy at heart. I know, for I've borrowed from him with nowt but my good name for security. Charlie turned the register round. "Sean MacNamara," he exclaimed. "Not him again!"

I was more than a little interested in Sean MacNamara, indeed, in anyone who could command the respect of a whole side of bacon. Somehow or other I must wheedle, persuade, bully, browbeat, procure, cajole, or coax his secret from him, perhaps through the medium of alcoholic beverage; though judging from his complexion, that would cost me a pretty penny.

During the meal, I had ample time and opportunity to examine further my 'victim.' On the wall in front of me was a mirror angled just right for my spying, in between dropping my mutton pie dinner onto my lap. A fat lot of good it did me for I was no nearer approaching the man nor was I any nearer his secret.

I could have saved myself the trouble though, for in the saloon bar after dinner, he sidled up to me. "Oi saw yah watching me just now," he said fiercely.

"Ah ... well, yes ... I ...er ... I thought I knew you." It was the best I could do on the spur of the moment.

"Oh!" he said licking his lips.

I took the hint. "What'll you have Mr ... er?"

"MacNamara, but my friends call me Sean. Oi'll have a whiskey with a Guinness chaser, if yah don't moind, sorr."

I gulped at the thought for I felt obliged to have the same to avoid crossing him.

He mellowed a bit towards me after his second drink and through casual conversation, by my way of it, I found that he had crossed from Ireland just that day, "after moi dear father's funeral," and he put on a suitably soulful expression and brushed an imaginary tear from his eye. His moustache drooped lower into his drooping mouth into his dripping Guinness.

"I thought you would be upstairs guarding your side of bacon," I said trying to bring in the subject in a casual manner, so to speak.

He looked up quickly from his drink, his little beady eyes staring at me. "And how did yah know about that?" The careful suspicious manner of his voice made me tread warily. I tried to be casual. "I was signing in same time as you," and waited.

He thought this over for a moment. "And yah didn't know moi name then?" He was most suspicious but luckily his drink ran out at that point and I ordered some more. "Oi'l pay, sorr," and he looked wryly at some small change in his hand, some very small change.

"No, no!" I hastily assured him, "The treat's on me tonight." I almost blushed when I thought of my motives.

MacNamara settled with his drink once more. "Moi bacon and moi sugar are quite safe." He patted his pocket where he evidently kept his room key.

I sat thinking up new line of attack, frantically rejecting one idea after another. "Food's getting pretty scarce now," I ventured.

At last he took the bait. "Well, it is and it isn't. It all depends on who yah know. Oi mean, it's not everybody that can buy a soide o' bacon, now, is it!" He became wary again perhaps sorry at his indiscretion.

I fished again. "The food situation can't be so bad in Ireland?" It was more a question than a statement.

He sipped his Guinness. "Depends." He stared down at the frothy head. "If yah know the roight people, 'tis alroight. Me sister Kate's married to a grocer, ya see ... O'Malley's Store ... a noice drop o' Guinness that."

I took the hint for I was getting somewhere at last now that the alcohol was talking. A sip of his fresh drink and he was off.

"Moi family roots are in Ballymana on the Mayo coast . . . maybe yah know the place?" I shook my head. "Oi've been over there at moi dear father's funeral" . . . dramatic pause . . . "Just dropped in to O'Malley's for some twist. Well, for sure, I got the surprise o' me loife. The place was stacked from floor to roof with bags o' sugar and soides o' bacon and fags and . . . oi've never seen so much stuff in all me loife. As for the prices, cheaper than the shops, sorr, cheaper than the shops."

He sipped his Guinness and leaned back in his seat to observe the effect of his story. "Where did it all come from then?" I asked tentatively.

"Moi very words sorr, moi very words. Well moi sister Kate told me. A food ship, it was, went down in the bay sunk boi the Germans."

I thought this one over for a bit as he finished his Guinness. Something didn't seem quite right and then it struck me. "How come the sugar didn't get wet?"

The Irishman blinked a bit and thought for a time as he pushed his empty glass away. "Oi can see that you're pretty astute, sorr, but I don't know that I should give yah the whole story, for O'Malley's sake, yah understand," he added mysteriously. Again I took the hint and arranged another refill.

"Very koind, thank ya sorr." He lifted his glass and toasted me.

"Yah see, it's like this, sorr. Old O'Malley was in cahoots with a U-boat captain. He had a weakness for Schnapps, had O'Malley ever since he had been on the Dutch Run in Kelley's coaster. The German captain would look out for lone stragglers of low tonnage and shadow them. Just about dusk, he would surface and order the crew to take to the boats and then tow his capture in the dark to Ballymana Bay using his diesels of course. O'Malley would meet him in the bay and unload what he could before dawn. The Germans then opened the seacocks and sank the prize. No sound, no torpedoes used up and a cut of the profits for the captain."

MacNamara filled in the long silence with a lengthy draught from his glass. I was so astounded by the whole scheme that I could think of nothing to say for a time. "He must have made a packet by now," I stuttered eventually but not before his Guinness had run out.

He stared at his empty glass and muttered, "Money, oh oi, money."

So I had the glass refilled. It would be worth it with such a source of grub within my grasp.

He brightened and opened out again. "O'Malley's a great one for the money. Very canny too. Didn't put it in a bank where the revenue boys could get their hands on it. Me sister Kate said that he had buried it away somewhere."

"Well, I can tell you straight, Mr MacNamara . . . "

"Sean. Yah can call me Sean, sorr."

"Er . . . Sean, that I wouldn't mind a side of bacon myself. Just how can I find this O'Malley's store?" I asked.

His eyes twinkled over the edge of his glass. "If I was you, sorr, I'd make for Stranraer . . . the crossing's still open and then from Belfast, the train to . . . " Then followed a whole rigmarole of train changes and a catalogue of small towns ending with Ballymana. " . . . but you'd better be quick, sorr. The stocks are gittin" a bit low."

"The convoys'll be getting more careful, I expect," I put in.

"More than that, sorr, more than that. The navy got wise to the Jerry captain and surprised him one morning in Ballymana Bay. The frigate came round Mayo Point and caught the U-boat on the surface. She dived and scooted away along the sandy bottom. Old

Jerry forgot something though, the prize ships he'd sunk. One hulk ripped the U-boat from stem to stern and that was the end of O'Malley's supplies – sort of poetic justice, you could call it."

"Still, he'll have made his fortune by now," I suggested.

"No doubt, now, there yah have a point, only O'Malley was on board the U-boat at the toime. He had a hankering for German gin, you know."

"Well, his widow will have a fortune then," I insisted.

"Ah well, yah see, he didn't tell Kate where he kept the money so she's just makin' what little she can on the remaining stock."

"Here! Have another beer and tell me again how to get to O'Malley's store . . ."

** *

The next morning, or rather day for it was late when I woke, I opened my eyes to find old Charlie Dank shaking me. As he came into focus, I could see and hear the glass of Seltzer he held in one hand – I told you he was kind hearted.

"Here, take this," he suggested as I groaned and tried to shut my sticky, rheumy eyes again. "It's time you were up and had some breakfast." I've never liked the word 'breakfast' but now it turned my gut completely upside down. "Bacon and eggs." I could just picture the grease and groaned again.

"You had a right merry time last night, you and that Irishman," Charlie went on. "I've been hearing things about him."

I opened wide my eyes. "Oh yes!"

"Yep! One of the commercial travellers recognised him. Said he was a regular cadger. Irish had a line he was shooting about getting hold of food easily and reckoned he could get boozed up every night on it if he wanted to."

I was really awake by this time. The cold shock of my feet on the lino reached my dull brain. "But the side of bacon and . . . and the sugar . . .?"

"Just his stage props."

"Stage props?"

"Yes! A bag of sawdust and a *papier mâché* lump of bacon."

And Charlie Dank laughed till the tears streamed down his cheeks when he saw my face and realised.

The Contract

All this happened in the late 1960s when a million pounds meant something, money was pre-decimal and computer programs were written on punched cards.

MacKenzie was a dried up stick of a young man. As he leant against the solid mahogany of an ancient bar, one foot on the brass rail and the rest of his six foot two on the polished top, the dim light from a beer advert. cast long shadows from his features.

Not that they were not long to begin with. His prominent parrot beak stuck out between the deep grooves that supported his chin. As for his eyes, they were lost somewhere under the shaggy ginger eyebrows and only emerged to check the state of the glass in his hand, a massive knobbly hand. All in all, his face would have reflected a sense of inner calmness, were it not for the occasional involuntary twitch at the corner of his mouth or the slight trembling of the sleeves of his Harris Tweed jacket.

It was almost two that afternoon when a rather rotund man with a ready smile and a thin scrape of hair over his almost bald pate bounced across the bar-room floor to where MacKenzie was ensconced.

"I thought I'd find you here, MacKenzie, old boy."

MacKenzie started and swung round to face the newcomer. "Oh, it's you," he growled, his accent betraying his northern home.

"Yes, of course it is. It's me, Ronny Clay. Who did you think it was?" Some of the bonhomie had left the newcomer. "What are you drinking, Colin?" he went on trying to retrieve the situation, for in actual fact these two were friends of longstanding – well, on and off they were, for their temperaments had clashed before this.

"Ah'll have another Glen Grant, Ronny," MacKenzie suggested relenting a bit.

"What, whiskey at this time of day!" But Clay refrained from further comment. He could see the signs rekindling under the bushy eyebrows.

The two men carried their whiskey and export to an alcove table in a cosy corner of the room, for although the pub was almost deserted, it was obvious that MacKenzie would open out more in privacy. It was clear that something was troubling him.

"Well, Colin old boy, what's up? Lose a million pounds or something?"

MacKenzie looked up and grinned wryly. "You could say that. Aye, you could say that." But he would say no more.

Clay tried another tack. "I see there's a bit in the Times here about Prof. Petraschen – he's an old colleague of yours, isn't he – they call him the million dollar brain . . . "

"Million pound brain," MacKenzie corrected.

Clay consulted his newspaper again. "By Jove, you're right, Col," and continued to read the article.

Colin Mackenzie's face rarely betrayed any emotion, but now there was some inner struggle taking place. "Listen Ronny!" – the other looked up from his newspaper – "We've known each other quite a time now . . ." He paused and licked his lips. The whiskey glass trembled.

"Go on, old boy." Clay felt it would all come out now.

"It was you mentioning Prof. Petraschen just now that brought it all back to mind."

A likely story, thought Clay but refrained from commenting. Instead, he merely nodded his head.

"You see," MacKenzie went on, "I used to work a lot with Petraschen. We were both under contract to the Universal

Computer Company. In fact, it was through U.C.C. that I first met Burt Petraschen."

** *

It would be last April when I was called into C.J. Coleman's office – you probably know C.J., the managing director of U.C.C. Well, as you can guess, I was astounded that he should even want to see me, for I had only been working on routine stuff up till then. Indeed at the time, I was working on some shipping schedules for a twelve berth port and had just completed the computer program. It still had to be tested, but it was hardly top line stuff worthy of a director's attention.

Nevertheless, there I was seated comfortably in a large leather chair drinking some foul sherry and smoking an equally foul cigar. C.J. opened up then and gave me the lowdown on some job he had lined up for me. "I'm afraid it will necessitate you going abroad," the pompous ass said; "Switzerland to be exact."

I nodded my agreement and reluctantly swallowed more of his eight-shilling-a-bottle sherry. The brown paper wad in my other hand had long become defunct.

"You are to become personal assistant to Professor Petraschen who unfortunately is ill at present. You will find him at this address," C.J. tossed over a paper, "one of the best clinics in the world."

I picked up the paper and quickly scanned it. "And what will be my duties, Sir?" I called him Sir for the job looked definitely attractive now. As you know, Petraschen is one of the top, no, *the* top brain in the computer world today.

C.J. continued: "Professor Petraschen has been rather ill for some time now and it is necessary that someone with sufficient technical knowledge should act as his secretary, or rather as his amanuensis. He is unable to write but his brain is perfectly clear and he is most willing to work."

I might say that I was more than a little shocked that the company should be wringing the last drop from someone so ill, no matter how valuable his knowledge might be. I started saying so to C.J. but he brushed my stuttering aside.

"I suppose I'd better give you some more background on the situation," he sighed in exasperation, "for I see that you seem to be shocked by our attitude; and if you're shocked now, there's no saying how you will react when you see the man."

"We, in the Universal Computer Company," he continued in his most intolerably egotistical fashion, "recognised the great talents of Professor Petraschen as long ago as 1954 and decided to try and tie him by contract for a period. Unfortunately, from our point of view of course, *he* also recognised his abilities and did a pretty shrewd bit of bargaining with us. The contract, however, was duly witnessed and signed – that's a copy if you wish to examine it – what it says is this." C.J. paused and cleared his throat for an important announcement, important in his eyes: "The Company (that's U.C.C) agrees to pay the undersigned, B. Petraschen, the sum of one million pounds to be paid in advance for the contract of his services for the following forty years or until his decease, whichever is the sooner."

Old C.J. spoke like an insurance policy but I hardly noticed. He had paused to let the significance of the contract sink in. Prof. Petraschen was contacted for forty years for a million quid in advance. A million quid!

"I believe that he meant to enjoy himself whilst he was young," C.J. continued. "We in turn mean to keep him alive until he fulfils his side of the bargain – another twenty-five years."

I just lay back in the leather chair, for the moment speechless, but I can't say I was very taken with the idea myself. I thought of my own contract at home, the one I'd never bothered to read, and began to wonder how many years I was committed as Petraschen's personal assistant – twenty-five years, perhaps?

At last I found my voice: "What exactly is he suffering from?"

Coleman hesitated before answering. Perhaps he was deciding just how much more he aught to tell me, for no doubt he could see just how I was accepting or rejecting the situation in its present state. Eventually he said: "He has severe cirrhosis of the liver with considerable amount of lung cancer in an advanced stage."

He turned away from me to show that the interview was at an end and yet somehow I got the impression that there was more to it, that he had not given me the complete story. Even so, the fact that Petraschen was about to pop off after enjoying their million quid cheered me up somewhat – you don't get cirrhosis of the liver through drinking lemonade.

** *

Two days later, the company plane was touching down at Vevey airport with only me and my luggage on board. I was quickly hustled through customs and from there led to a Rolls with the

U.C.C. crest on the side. They were certainly treating me in style. I'd better check my contract again.

The clinic itself was a very pleasant single storey building extending down three sides of a square. Within the square was an admin. building with a small emergency powerhouse attached. The whole setting was Swiss-chaletish enhanced perhaps by the projecting eaves of the buildings forming a verandah running round most of the structure.

A keeper of the small chalet lodge informed the main building of our arrival and I was greeted by the director of the clinic, Herr Doktor Kopftergrassen – I just called him Herr Doktor after the first few attempts. He was virtually the popular concept of a Japanese with his large grey head bobbing up and down in welcome and a face wreathed in smiles to show the finest set of stainless steel teeth I've ever seen – but why the German name?

But appearances can be deceptive for I saw some of his work later and there was no doubt at all as to his ability as a surgeon.

"Of course, you will want to rest, Mr MacKenzie." He relieved me of a handgrip. "Your quarters are over this way. Follow me, please." He even had the nasal quality of the Japanese. Maybe he was Japanese with a German name. I never ever found out.

My quarters were austere but comfortable enough for all that with even a colour tele. The reception was never very good on that particular set; besides, my French had never been very good either. There were six male doctors in the hospital and one female whom I gather was a biologist. I call them male and female for although we all fed together in a little dining room, that was all I ever found out about them.

They were singularly uncommunicative even to the point of being rude and even aggressive towards me. Herr Doktor explained this away by saying that there was some disagreement at present with certain policies. Yet, I could not help but feel that the aggression was directed against me personally and had nothing to do with internal strife.

Next day, I was taken to meet my mentor, Professor Petraschen. I had steeled myself for this meeting although luckily I had had very little time to think about it. I don't know what I imagined it would be like but certainly I never expected the situation which greeted my eyes.

Petraschen was lying in a small bed near the window. His form never moved as I entered the room and his eyes remained fixed on the ceiling. This "greeting" did not particularly surprise me. What did surprise me, however, was the vast array of equipment in his room. Since I was to work there, I half expected the desk computer and the card-punching machine; even the overhead projector did not seem superfluous for presumably he could not move his head and therefore used the ceiling for all his reading. Nor did the appearance of the man himself shock me. When I got into his visual range he smiled and greeted me cheerfully enough in a peculiar croaking voice: "Do come in, Mr MacKenzie, and let me look at you." Petraschen's eyes scanned me up and down.

"Good day, Professor. I must say you are looking well." Indeed he did look well. This produced a great silent laugh from Petraschen causing him to draw his lips away from his clenched teeth and even produced a tear or two. An attendant nurse wiped away the tear almost mechanically – so he must be completely paralysed, I thought. "I believe you and I are going to be companions for a bit," Petraschen croaked on. "You might as well find your way around this junk," and his rolling eyes indicated what he meant.

I wandered my way between pieces of equipment examining them with feigned interest, for mathematics and not machines is my life. I was suddenly aware that half the machines in the room were keeping the man alive. A small double peristaltic pumping unit was, in effect, an artificial heart pumping his life's blood to a synthetic membrane artificial lung which rolled with drunken motion through some cam arrangement in one corner of the room.

I now recognised an artificial kidney machine, not in operation at that moment, with several other pieces of dormant equipment that were new to me. The integrated setup was monitored by several chart recorders ticking away on a panel – this one monitored blood pressure; that one oxygen content of blood – the man was a living machine. Petraschen saw my face as I returned to the desk beside his bed. "It's shocking, don't you think?" He drew his lips over his clenched teeth once more to give his leering impression of a smile. "Of course, you realise they are simply keeping me alive to use my brain. We might as well get started and give them their money's worth. They keep telling me how much the equipment costs and what with my original contract – you know about that, I expect – they must have spent a bomb on me already."

Again he dissolved into silent mirth with tears streaming down his temples and into his hair before the nurse wiped them away. I think I understood the joke but it hardly raised what you would call a belly laugh.

I sat down at the desk and tried out the various gadgets there. All worked perfectly, an unusual thing in itself.

"Well, what's the current project, then?" the Prof. asked. And so we got down to work on the petroleum company's new refinery and twelve berth port that I had already started.

That first day's work was the greatest strain for me – the continual background slogging of pumps and the hissing of recorders – the Prof. staring at the ceiling most of the time – the annoying fussiness of the nurse although she never altered the controls of the various life machines; I reckon that they must have been completely automated.

Nevertheless, Petrachen completed and checked my previous month's work in a mere morning. I was completely deflated and told him so. I expect it gave him considerable pleasure to realise that at least his brain was still functioning as a top class unit.

The following day and thereafter, we were left alone together without the distraction of the nurse. My guess is that either C.J. or Petraschen pleaded the importance of secrecy in our work; Petraschen seemed particularly pleased so I think he was the one responsible. Anyway, it says a lot for their confidence in their machinery. I remember one day the heart pump failed. There was almost immediately a click and a standby unit came into action as alarm bells sounded faintly in the distance.

Within thirty seconds, three technicians or doctors (I don't know which) were in the room and within one minute the faulty pump had been slipped out of line and replaced with a new one. They had every cause to be confident. Petraschen said enigmatically: "If I go, they go!" and grinned.

"What's the project today, then, Colin?" Petraschen and I were on first name terms now.

"Well Burt, there is this distillation set-up for the separation of six hydrocarbons." We were still working on the refinery project. "We have to use the Ponchon and Savarit method so I have here the enthalpy data, but I'm afraid there is no equilibrium information. Shall we use Raoult's law and combine this into a six dimensional analysis with enthalpy as one dimension . . ." The technical jargon flowed on as we knocked a relatively simple programme into shape.

At one point, Burt Petraschen broke off and stared at the ceiling for a long period: "It's very cold, Colin, very cold." I lifted a spare blanket and spread it over him even though to me the central heating seemed abominably hot. The movement caught his eye and snapped him back to his former self; for he gave a silent chuckle as though amused at some private joke.

It must have been just about then that I started sleeping badly. At first, I put this down to the high altitude for I had headaches with my insomnia. What was more significant, however, was the way in which my thoughts seemed continually occupied with my mentor, Petraschen. I began to wonder what he really thought of all the laboured efforts to keep him alive just to fulfil his million pound contract. At first it seemed to him as one huge joke but as time went on, his spells of preoccupation grew longer and more frequent. The cold particularly bothered him in spite of, as I said, the hot atmosphere in his room. No doubt, the artificial heart was not keeping his circulation up to scratch.

One afternoon (we did not work in the afternoons) I mentioned the cold to Herr Doktor suggesting that the artificial heart was not doing its job properly. He stared at me as though I were mad and mumbled something about doing what he could. Thereafter, Herr Doktor was noticeably more distant and in spite of his efforts, Petraschen was still cold.

I like to think of my free time as my own; yet somehow I got it into my head that Burt Petraschen was my responsibility and that it was up to me to keep, if not his body, his spirits healthy. I took to paying him social calls in the afternoons with this in mind and after a short period, we became quite close friends on an intellectual plane.

He loved to talk, mainly of the riotous times he had with the million pound down payment and how the excesses of his living had brought ruin to his body yet leaving his brain as sharp and clear as ever it had been. His first breakdown was cirrhosis of the liver; that was about five years ago. More recently, this lung trouble came to the surface and through operation, one lung was completely removed. Since then it was one thing after another although he refused to talk about his more recent medical history. I think it gave him the horrors. And throughout it all, the infernal cold of his body.

After tiring myself out in the evenings with some private work – I was writing a book of problems at the time – I would drop into bed and pull the large bolster-type eiderdown over me. In the darkness, I could picture Petraschen lying in his cot, struggling with teeth clenched against the pain and cold of his body. In my brain, this continuous clicking and hissing of nervous recorders and the gentle chug chug, slurp slurp of the pumps, growing in volume until the great crescendo of sound almost overwhelmed me and I would sit bolt upright in the darkness with sweat trickling down my neck and my pyjama jacket clinging to my back. The crazy thought went through my mind that the heat of Burt's body had been transferred to my own.

It was association of ideas, I suppose, but it was then that I began wondering why I was really in that clinic. A source of spare parts? I switched on the light and looked at myself in the mirror. I almost laughed. Me for spare parts? They couldn't have chosen a more decrepit specimen. It was a disquieting thought just the same and after this contract business, I would not put anything past C.J. and his cronies. Needless to say, I didn't get a lot of sleep that night in spite of the chair under the door handle.

On the Saturday of that same week, quite a remarkable change came over Petraschen. I had never heard a mention of pain from the man, but now his brow was furrowed and his teeth more tightly clenched than ever.

"Colin," he cried when he saw me, "it's maggots . . . maggots . . . I can feel them all over me. Kill them, man, kill them;" and he started moaning in a most peculiar rasping way. I tried to comfort him and laid my hand on his brow, his wet and clammy brow, sticky and clinging like a fillet of fish. The touch soothed him and the morning's work restored his humour. Before I left for lunch he murmured, "Thanks Colin," and his eyes glistened.

I determined to make that afternoon one of my social visits for it seemed that Petraschen needed the company; besides, if anyone knew about nefarious spare part filching he would. I suppose I could have left it there and then, but it's part of my heritage to see a job through to its end; or you can put it down to stubbornness, perhaps even stupidity.

Anyway, that afternoon we talked about ethics with me trying to swing the conversation to spare part surgery. He was for none of it, however, for he talked mainly about the sanctity of life and the rights and wrongs of suicide.

"You know, Colin," he said, "if I had the courage and the power I should be dead by now." While I was puzzling over that one, he added; "What's your attitude to euthanasia, Col?"

I stared at him and murmured some self-righteous thing about living out ones natural lifespan. *"Dum spiro spero . . ."*

"Hope! Hope! There's no hope for me, man," he spat out and closed his eyes.

I got up to leave and I think the sound caught his attention for he opened his eyes once more. "Don't go yet, Col lad." He paused for a moment. "I have a proposition to put to you." I sat down again but avoided his eyes in the embarrassment of the moment.

"Listen, Colin. I want you to kill me." Then seeing my shock: "put me to rest, to sleep . . . euthanasia . . . call it what you will." There was a long pause. I didn't know what to say and I just stared at him. I think my mouth was open. "In that top drawer," he indicated with his eyes, "you will find the key to a deposit box. If you promise to kill me, I'll tell you the bank and the box number. There is an authorisation card there too . . ." and he mumbled on about some other technicalities.

Observing my silence, he smiled in his peculiar grim way and said: "Think about it."

I think I would have left at that point, not only his room but the clinic itself. I'm no saint, as you well know, but neither am I a murderer nor a euthanasiast or whatever it is. His eyes darted up to the ceiling with a blind stare somewhere between stark terror and panic. "Damn them," he hissed, "it's those damned maggots." His eyes turned to me pleading: "Please, Col, please." My hand returned to the clamminess of his forehead and soothed him before I fled for the sanctuary of my own room.

What a proposition! My first reaction was to reject it out of hand. Yet lying wakeful in my bed that night, nagging doubts assailed me. Was it fair to keep the man alive, to keep him to his million pound bargain? On the other hand, I couldn't quit the clinic and go back to U.C.C. to tell C.J. that his big cheese had maggots; and no doubt, if I abandoned the company, C.J. would make sure that I stayed unemployed for the rest of my days – he had hinted as much at that last meeting.

Through the fog of doubts and counter doubts came the file-rasp cry of "maggots" with the steady beat beat beat of the heart pump which seemed to synchronise with my own heart pump thumping in my ear drums. The sounds kept eddying around my brain and echoed off into space as I fell down through my mind's fog. Far below, staring up at me from his cot prison I saw Burt Petraschen, that same look of terror in his eyes that had transfixed me earlier. Falling, falling nearer and yet no nearer, for each time I seemed about to strike the figure in the bed, it reappeared again just as far away . . . falling faster, each cycle repeatedly faster . . . I hit the cot and woke up screaming to the sound of falling furniture.

The overhead light in my bedroom showed the anxious faces of two of the medical staff. A chair was lying on its side, the chair I had fixed under the door handle. My mind was made up.

Sunday was a rest day for Burt Petraschen and me. I slept late after the ructions of the previous night. My mind was still made up.

I entered Petraschen's room with a brusque, "Good morning, Burt."

He looked slightly puzzled and frowned as I refused to sit down but paced to and fro in the restricted room available at the foot of the bed. "Well?" he asked.

"I've made my decision, Burt." His face cleared. "I . . . I . . ." My hesitation caused him to frown again. "I just can't do it, Burt." I cut his pleading short. "It's just no good. I know you've had a bit of a raw deal but I have some loyalty to U.C.C. You must have too or you would just refuse to work for them. Can't you ask them for a spell off, or offer to return that money in the safely deposit to cancel the contract?"

"You don't understand, Colin man. I just don't want to go on living." A tear tickled down his temple on to the pillow.

For a time we were both silent, me pacing up and down and him motionless with his eyes closed. Petraschen broke the silence: "Can I make one last appeal, Col, please? Please!"

I nodded curtly.

"Lift the blankets then and see what you are keeping alive." I hesitated a long moment, then made to protest. "Go on, man, go on," he cried.

I stepped forward to raise the blankets and stared for a full long minute before I dropped them back in place. Without a word, I turned and strode over to the heart pump placing one hand on the rheostat knob. I turned it hard to the right. The pump raced and in the distance I could hear alarm bells before I turned the control to its original position. As the attendants raced in, I was standing there looking at his calm serene face marred only by the trickle of blood from one nostril.

** *

MacKenzie looked up from his drink avoiding the eyes of his companion.

"It says here he died from a stroke, old boy," said Clay uneasily.

MacKenzie nodded: "Mmm. The increased pump pressure did it." He swilled down the rest of the amber liquid and played with the empty glass between his two hands before going over to the bar and ordering the same again.

Clay moved uncomfortably searching for something to say: "Much money in the deposit box, Col?"

MacKenzie sipped his drink: "Dunno. He never told me its number."

Again silence.

"It must have been horrible, Col, horrible. Were there . . . maggots, Col? What was under the blankets, Col?"

Colin MacKenzie emptied his glass. "There was nothing, nothing at all."

"No maggots?" Clay sounded disappointed.

MacKenzie looked the other straight in the eye. "Nothing. No body. Nothing but a wire cage and some plastic tubes . . . only a head . . . a million pound brain."

Old Dave's Talisman

It is said that an Irishman has small stomach for the English; the Scot hardly tolerates his Sassenach neighbour; the Saxon and the Welsh have a mutual repulsion. And the Yorkshireman? He hates just about everyone.

Old Dave Charlton was a Yorkshireman. I say 'was', for he passed away last March about a week after that bad fall of snow. They buried him fifteen feet down in Thorndyke Cemetery – the first nine feet was snow. He would have liked that, would old Dave.

At that time, things were not going too well for me and I was reduced to managing his hill farm on account of him and his bad heart. Not that the farm job was bad in itself. It was his continual bickering about little things – the cost of a roll of wire – a dozen stakes – a kilo of U-staples. He liked to think he still ran things in spite of being bedridden with his heart condition. A knock of his walking stick on the bedroom floor would summon Meg Regan – she kept house for him – and through her he would convey his instructions, or fetch his minions to his bedside. His minions! Ha, there's a laugh for a start; for besides myself and Meg, there was only young Jim Clough who was usually away at the Back O' the Hill bothy, and Dave's nephew, Jacky Green.

Now Jackie had his own little business, ten miles or so down the dale towards Whitby, where he just managed to scrape a living by making and selling agricultural chemicals. Actually all he seemed to do was to buy in raw materials and mix them together. Mind you, he knew what he was doing all right for he could – and did – write B.Sc. (failed) after his name. Still, I don't reckon business was all that good. The farmers preferred to buy from the big firms rather than risk his hand-labelled bottles of sheep dip and what-have-you.

Perhaps his salesmanship manner was at fault, for he had the same mean streak as his uncle Dave. Some evenings, the two of them would spend the long hours in Old Dave's bedroom shouting at each other in language fit to curl Meg's very straight hair. I can picture it yet: Meg and I huddled over the kitchen fire with the fires o' Hell roaring in the bedroom overhead; Old Dave propped up in bed, his face lined with a fine purple network of broken veins, his eyes lost beneath hairy coat-hanger eyebrows which seemed to support a grotesque false nose with quivering bristles from its nostrils, a great enormous gash of a mouth continually chewing or gnashing or spitting over some difference of opinion with his syncopated dentures. The nephew had the same beetle brows but as yet had time on his side so that in contrast, his face seemed white next to the old man's. Nevertheless, Jacky's choice of epithets was more than equal to his uncle's, a reflection on his corporate university life.

"I don't like the sound of this at all, Josh," Meg remarked one evening. "The old man'll have another heart attack with all this upset."

"Oh don't worry yourself, lass. You know how he thrives on this sort of thing. Besides he got those pills from Doc. Alexander to keep him quiet." It wasn't the old man she was thinking of, though; she had a job and a roof over her head to consider.

Suddenly, all was quiet overhead. I knew the signs for it had happened before. Jacky had given the old man his tranquilisers to shut him up. I could hear the creak of the floorboards as the younger man moved around and eventually a door slammed and we could hear Jacky's boots clatter down the staircase. He looked furious when he poked his head round the kitchen door. "I'm off t' bloody Crown 'n Anchor," he stated and waited as though expecting an answer.

“Don’t be too late, for your uncle’s sake,” Meg suggested and I smirked at the thought.

A scowl, another door wracked and Jacky was gone. Just as well too for I had a bit of a thirst coming on and I knew where Meg kept her private supply of stout. I knew too that she wouldn’t be inclined to share it, what with him in the offing.

An hour later with the two of us huddled round the fire, a glass each of stout and a red-hot poker – for the cold of the night was closing in – we were started from our reverie by a god almighty bang.

It came from upstairs.

Meg looked at me and I looked at Meg while I made up my mind to go up and investigate. Now you can understand that I didn’t decide all too quickly, for that surely sounded like a shotgun and most shotguns have two barrels. We listened, but not a sound, not the creak of a board nor the yawn of a tired-out timber; only the sough of the wind and a death’s rattle of hail against the window pane.

Through no choice of mine, I led the way upstairs to Old Dave’s bedroom. The door was yet closed. I squeaked it carefully open. The light streamed out and blinded me for a moment until my pupils dilated to a slow realisation that Dave was lying there among distraught bedclothes, staring at something imaginary hanging from the ceiling. His mouth was distorted to an indescribable leer by the thick tense cords of his neck muscles. Dave was dead.

* * *

" ... and this here is Detective Inspector Bradshaw from Northallerton to make enquiries about t'shooting business." It was hours later and our local constable, Bobby Clark (I don't know if Bobby was his real name), was introducing us in his own canny way, for he was evidently relieved that someone with higher authority had come in to take over the investigation. "T' Inspector's going to ask a few questions."

The Inspector looked at each of us in turn, Meg, Jacky and myself. We stared back at him in silence. I remembered being fascinated by two bristling hairs protruding from a mole on his cheek. It's funny but the rest is just a grey face from the past ... and it was only last March.

This is a most mysterious affair," the Inspector barked. It was a bad beginning letting the opposition (that is to say the three of us) know that he was puzzled too. "We'll start with you, Mr Green." He turned to Jacky.

"Don't ye want t'see's alone then," Jacky queried?

"Nope. Prefer to be open and above board with my enquiries. Plenty of time later for private statements." He managed to get a sly nuance into his last phrase. "You I believe, are the dead man's nephew. I suppose too that you will inherit (pause) this place;" again the sly inference.

Jacky moved uncomfortably. "I was down at Crown an' Anchor when it happened, you know," he muttered. "No use askin' me anything. You can check if y' like."

The inspector nodded his head sagely and scribbled something in his notebook. I diverted my fascination from his mole to the half glass of flat stout on the mantelpiece and all the while I could hear the scratching of the pencil. Everyone seemed to be holding their breath.

I struggled to concentrate on the matter and automatically pulled my pipe from my pocket. "Dunno Inspector." I frowned in an effort at recollection. "Mrs Regan phoned straight away, if that's any help ... "

"That was 8.13pm, sir," Bobby Clark interrupted. "I took the call myself."

More scratching in the notebook . . . and so the questions went on. Did I know this and that . . . had he any enemies (what a question to ask about Old Dave Charlton). . . who prepared his meals . . . what did he eat . . . he'll be saying next that his dinner exploded. Then with the air of someone playing his trump card, the inspector laid a long thin object before me. "Recognise that?"

With my briar, I poked the thing gingerly over and over on the table and frowned again. It appeared to be a length, a yard or so, of red rubber tubing knotted at both ends. A long slit ran almost from one knot to the other. "Aye! I've seen it before. It was hanging in the old man's bedroom when we went in." Somewhere in the recesses of my mind a memory stirred. Somewhere I had seen this in some other context, some other situation, some other time.

"I've seen't too," Jacky put in. "There's a story behind it that goes back to his early days with farm. The old man kept it as a reminder of the days when he used it to syphon paraffin from his neighbours' tractors to use in his own . . . tractors ran on paraffin in those days. He thought of it as his lucky charm, so to speak. He asked me to hang it on his wall. It made him laugh at the thought."

The inspector opened his eyes in mock wonderment and I must say I felt a little puzzled myself. I didn't think the old man was sentimental about things and certainly not superstitious.

"The rubber was wet when I arrived, sir. Seems to have dried quickly." Constable Clark had to get his neb in. Bradshaw silenced him with a glare. He would brook no interference and I had the vague uneasy feeling that this inspector would solve no dark mysteries this dark evening. Perhaps a little bit of help from me wouldn't go wrong. I started thinking hard.

The remainder of that first collective interview went over my head and I believe Inspector Bradshaw noticed my abstraction, for later when he was leaving and I was seeing the two of them off the premises, he drew me aside.

"And why all the deep thoughts, Mr Coles," nice and friendly like?

By this time I had it all worked out, or so I thought. I told him my theory with certain chosen blanks, of course, and how we could trap the murderer; for by now I think we all concluded that murder had been done.

He looked at me stonily. He was thinking hard too. "Well Mr Coles, I expect the inquest will be on Wednesday the 27th. Don't forget! Wednesday. I'll see you all then."

***

Wednesday arrived.

Meg, true to form made up sandwiches for the three of us and packed them individually in case we were separated. Not that we expected any arrests but you never know. I put Jacky's in his little attaché case, Meg's were in her basket and I stuffed mine into my overcoat pocket.

The inquest was a dreary affair. Meg and I gave our evidence of the discovery of the body and the inspector added a few more details.

Doctor Alexander had some interesting information to give. Apparently the old man had not been shot and a blood analysis showed that he had only taken the normal two-pill dose of his tranquilisers. The intriguing point about this medicine however was its effect on Old Man Charlton. It would have relaxed him completely, indeed so much so that he was virtually paralysed yet not asleep. He stated that the old man had simply died of heart failure and added that in his opinion, this had been precipitated by the loud bang we had heard. The coroner had this withdrawn . . . something about being based on evidence not yet on record.

It was then that things got moving. Inspector Bradshaw was recalled to the witness stand when a mighty bang rocked the courtroom. I recognised the sound and so did Meg. A very red-faced Jacky stood up with the remains of his attaché case before him. The lid had been blown completely away showing inside . . . a length of knotted tubing.

Meg stood up. "Jacky Green!" she accused as he made for the door.

I suppose there is a moral to this tale – you can be too clever.

You see I reckoned I knew what had happened that night. That piece of rubber tubing in Old Charlton's bedroom had been knotted at one end, filled with solid carbon dioxide - dry-ice they call it - and knotted at the other end. I can just picture it now. The length of tubing suspended above his head getting larger and larger as the solid carbon dioxide heated and changed to gas and Charlton lying in bed helplessly watching, unable to do anything, waiting for the tube to burst. The suspense alone probably killed the man. I remember this as a practical joke from my student days. You see, Jacky Green wasn't the only one with B.Sc. (failed) to his credit.

So here I am, Josh Coles, in prison awaiting trial for murder. You see, I was too clever by far. I knew too much and it was enough to set that dumb Inspector Bradshaw off on a few enquiries. To start with, the little trap I set in Jacky's case was enough to panic anyone let alone impetuous Jacky. It alerted the police to my background knowledge. Besides the timing of the device was far too precise for anyone with a mere passing knowledge. How did I know when the tube would burst. Perhaps I had tried this device in the past, which I had in my college days. Where did the dry-ice come from? What about the peculiar figure of 8 knots tied in the tubing, a relic of my boating days? The inspector demanded answers to all these questions, answers I could supply.

So here I am sitting on the concrete floor of my cell with my back against the bunk bed, humming a little tune from my past:

Sittin' alone in a boxcar's four walls

Because of a break in the rich man's laws …

…They took me to the jailhouse and now I must die.

Five hours to live boys, how the time does fly.

. . . well not quite that in this jurisdiction.

Why did I do it? Well, I'm a Yorkshireman too!

Haber's Ghost

Maybe you've heard of Pepper's Ghost. It's a 19th century stage device used in the old Victorian music halls to conjure up the illusion of a ghost. It used a combination of mirror and sheet glass as a basis; and very effective it was in those days before present-day electronic tricks you see on a TV screen. I don't know why I mention this for Haber's ghost has nothing to do with electronic ploys or Dr Pepper. Let me stop this rambling and start at the beginning.

It was my first job in the chemical industry. I had tried my hand working on a farm, a mixed farm with some corn and hay crops but mostly producing milk with a herd of Ayrshire cows; only I didn't fancy being poor for the rest of my days. I had even laboured in a brick works but that too was going nowhere. The chemical works job looked interesting and the money was good, leastways better than the others.

I was new to the task but I already had some laboratory skills from away back. My boss, Jack Karrer, showed me what he wanted, some routine menial tasks involving the main processing plant on the site, plant for producing ammonia. My job was to bring back samples from the plant for analysis in the laboratory.

Right from the start, I didn't take to the man. As you know, I wear glasses, the type with bulging lenses so that through them, straight lines always appear to bend in a bow. Jack Karrer was like that – never saw things straight. He had the sort of twisted mind-lens that not only bent things but twisted them into all sorts of fantasies. I was unaware of this to begin with but it manifested itself soon enough. He was picky over things, indeed over most things and I came to the conclusion that it was all there to hide his own lack of self-confidence. Anyway, the money was good.

Andy, one of the assistants, took me out to the main works area to show me the layout and also to introduce me to the building where I would be taking the samples. The building, aptly named the converter shed, was a long brick structure with a skeleton of a roof – open to the elements. Having worked on a farm, the so-called elements didn't bother me, but I did wonder about the roof. The converters themselves were enormous vertical tubes about 30 metres high and 1 metre in diameter, with several of these along the length of the building like the Parthenon – truly a majestic vista of columns. These vessels were cradled within cages of substantial steelwork and had flanged endplates leading various tubes into and out of the system. Enormous nuts kept the plates in place; I could not envisage any human hands lifting such large items far less fix and turn them. I had a look at the roof – or lack of roof – but made no comment. I was all agog.

Andy took me through a doorway (again no door) to an abutting brick structure with bundles of vertical tubes constantly being sprayed with water. It felt as though I was in the middle of some Eastern country in the monsoon season and thereafter I thought of the place as the Monsoon Room. He explained that the tubes were inter-stage heat exchangers (whatever that is) to cool the gases from the compressors in the next building before the gas were finally compressed and passed into the convertors to make ammonia. We hurriedly left this dismal place and entered the compressor room.

One of the compressors was stripped down for maintenance exposing its innards to the vulgar gaze, my vulgar gaze. It struck me right away what a beautiful piece of engineering lay before me, all shiny and precise. I could but admire this sculptured technology, the gearing and bearings of a work of art. I gazed at the pump for what seemed like an eternity. Andy prodded me on and back to the laboratory.

There, he outlined the industrial technique which apparently is called the Haber Process for manufacturing ammonia. The details were looted from the Germans after the First World War and operated with varying degrees of success. Essentially, nitrogen and hydrogen are compressed and pushed through a catalyst to give ammonia, as simple as that. Well, not as simple as that, for the system operates at high pressure (about 200bar) and the ammonia is liquefied at a later stage . . . nasty stuff. Their research project was to run the operation under different conditions to find the optimum set-up. I was beginning to get nervous. Still, the money was good.

At various times then through the day, I was given a couple of sample bottles - I think they are called Dreschel flasks - and a gas meter and told to run a couple of tests on Number X converter, note the time and main pressure etc. etc. and the leg number. I was going to ask if that was the inside leg or what then thought better of it. And each day I would do the tests. I would go in through the compressor room (my favourite place) via the Monsoon Room and into the convertor bay. I didn't linger long in the steamy jungle of the exchangers with the vague figure of someone brushing down the tubes (to discourage algae formation,

I believe). Amid the monsoon atmosphere and the ammonia fumes, I could hear his hacking cough. I paused once to say good day but there was no response. It wasn't a good day in that building or that atmosphere. I did wonder if he thought the money was good.

I soon settled down to the routine of the place. Jenny, another lab. assistant who worked on the same bench, gave me the lowdown on the setup. "Keep clear of Karrer, if you've any sense," she declared. "He's a crabby old git. If anything goes wrong, it's always someone else's fault," she spat out. I guessed he wasn't her favourite person.

One day I collected my meter and Dreschel as usual when she remarked, "Don't you use a lute?" I puzzled over this, wondering if I needed to sing as I sampled, sort of along the long highway of the converter shed; good name for a song but never a hit. "You need a safely valve, a lute, immediately after the sample line. Did no one say?" and seeing my confusion continued: " It's just a T-piece dipping into a cylinder of water. Old Karrer would have had your guts if he had seen that." I duly complied and a lute was added to my collection.

Passing through the Monsoon Room from the compressors, the figure in his stiff liquorice industrial water-proofs was busy as ever cleaning down the algae-covered tubes with his stiff bristle brush and coughing his lungs out as usual. As before, I greeted him with a good day only to be met by a blank stare. He wasn't one for much conversation - or for any conversation. I went about my routine; purge line through the reduction valve, this time connected the lute, then the Dreschel and finally the meter. This particular day, it was almost as bad as the Monsoon Room with the cold North Sea haar mixed with heavy rain pelting through the open roof. It was as quick as I could get through the tests and then out. It's time they got a roof on this building. I didn't see my oil-skinned friend as I rushed through and back to the lab.

After some wry (or should that be dry) comments from Jenny and a dry lab. coat, and with the steam wiped from my specs. I set about completing the tests; for now, I was allowed to do the analysis part. Nothing to it! Just a simple acid/base titration. I left the calculation part to Andy.

In the course of the following few weeks, I worked out the company set-up as well as the personnel structure. It all came down to Karrer being the boss I had to account to. For some reason, I got the feeling that he didn't really like me. I certainly didn't take to him. It's just as well the money was good. It was also the occasion when Jenny and I got quite chatty. I learned that she already had a boy friend; that hadn't stopped me in the past.

During our gossiping, talk got round to the converter premises and the bleakness of the site. "It's time they got round to putting a roof on the place," I commented. I had been soaked yet again.

"Oh, they stopped doing that some time ago," Jenny remarked. "The explosions kept blowing it off," and seeing my blank expression, "Didn't anyone tell you? They haven't got the process sussed out completely and every now and then one of the converters explodes. You'll know when that happens!" she remarked with some feeling. "The last time, three process workers were killed - just over a year since. Karrer should have told you."

Suddenly I felt that the money was not all that special.

I was extra careful with my tests after that, but you know how it is. You get accustomed to a situation no matter how dangerous and you think it couldn't happen to you. It's well recognised that the chemical industry is inherently dangerous; yet plenty of people are happily employed in chemical manufacturing. Nevertheless, I did take extra care.

One day during a test, the maintenance crew had just emptied the catalyst from one of the converters, a process which wasn't all that frequent. So for a time I stood and watched the operation. Some of the catalyst spilled over and onto the concrete floor. Out of curiosity, I picked up some of the material and had a good look at the small globules. They had all the appearance of chocolate raisins, dark plain chocolate, the type I like.

After a time, I left the scene and returned to the lab. to show my spoils to Jenny. "That's ebony oxide, some of the catalyst," she exclaimed. "You're not supposed to remove that from the site."

"But it's just iron oxide, isn't it?" I countered. "It's well known across the industry . . . no great secret."

"With some trace material added to make it more efficient," she qualified. "A big secret so don't let Karrer see you with it; dump it!" I did dump it in the waste bin *tout de suite*. She continued, "They'll be starting the reduction process soon on that new batch. It was during one of these when we had the last explosion. I think the explanation was that the whole process got too hot and distorted the flanges letting air mix with escaping gases . . . then boom. Everyone thought that Karrer had some explaining to do, but there was nothing forthcoming."

Some time after that, I had just completed taking some tests when the heavens opened and I had my customary drenching. I hurried out through the heat exchanger shed giving my usual wave to the figure in oilskins and accepted a returned nod of the head. I can tell you, I wasn't in the best of moods when I returned to the lab. with my steamed up glasses only to be greeted by Karrer with a smirk and a snide remark, "A great day for the ducks!"

I could feel my blood rising. Were it not for Jenny's presence, I might have blown a gasket. Instead, "Why can't I have bloody oilskins like him with the brush in that exchanger shed?" Karrer's reaction surprised me. He said not a word, only turned deathly pale and turned on his heel. I just stared after him.

The silence was broken by Jenny. "You've seen the ghost, then!"

"Ghost! You're kidding me. That was no ghost"

"Must have been. They don't have anyone doing that job now. It's all done by permanent pressure washers, besides you're not the only one to see it, you know. We call him Haber's Ghost." As I took this in, she went on, "We think it's one of the victims of the last explosion come back to haunt Karrer. He certainly took it to heart. You should have seen his face." I did see his face in spite of my specs.

Jack Karrer didn't mention this again; on the other hand, a suit of oilskins (for my use, no less) materialised in the laboratory not long after and I had a feeling that he made a point of avoiding me.

My job of work continued its dreary way and developed little beyond sample taking and simple titrations. One thing did change though. I no longer saw the ghost as I passed through the Monsoon Room. Maybe he was away on holiday haunting some other site. Do ghosts take holiday breaks? I did try to entice Jenny out for a local show. But no, she had a date with her boy-friend for that night! Besides, what would we talk about apart from burettes and pipettes? We really had nothing in common except Jack Karrer; I couldn't see that lasting more than five minutes, even less.

The tests continued; the titrations continued; the rain continued; and as for the tittle tattle, yes, it continued.

Then it happened! I walked over the yard to the compressor room and made for the monsoon chamber. There was the ghost again this time barring the way. He just stood in the doorway his arms waving frantically back and forth. I hesitated a big hesitation. I couldn't go past him and I certainly was not going to walk through him. I don't know what happened next. All I do know is that I woke up between white sheets with my ears ringing and a hospital odour up my nose. One hand was heavily bandaged and I was conscious of the faint ping of a heart monitor. A hazy unfamiliar face was bent over me. She said something that I couldn't quite make out, but I came to the conclusion that the face belonged to a nurse. I closed my eyes and drifted back into another world.

Peculiar dreams alongside curious figures meandered past. I even thought that I could discern my acquaintance, the ghost in the black shiny waterproofs. Again I drifted off and meandered aimlessly through a dreamland of exotic shapes and colours before falling into a pink paradise of nothingness.

Eventually I surfaced to focus on another ill-defined anonymous face, this time a doctor, I think. "You've had a lucky escape," she said as I drifted in and out of my cloudy paradise. "If you'd gone further into the room . . . " and the voice floated away.

After some time, I don't know how long, I became much more aware of my surroundings. I appeared to be alone in this room, not really alone, for there was a whole variety of machines and gadgets completely foreign to me and their blurred hieroglyphs meant nothing without my glasses.

I think I was getting better; I felt better in spite of the throbbing hand; and I was taking more interest in the pale green room. Do hospitals always have pale green decors? Perhaps the NHS got a job lot at a cut price.

My first visitor was Jenny. She came on an evening, probably straight from work and brought her boyfriend. After exchanging greetings, introductions and a peck on the forehead, she asked how I was. “Do you see my specs. around anywhere?” I asked; I felt naked without them. They were eventually found in a bedside drawer and I felt better.

We talked half-heartedly for a bit about work and how things in general were going. Eventually we got round to the explosion itself. “I'm surprised your glasses survived the blast. The Dreschel bottle didn't. I think it must have cut your hand on its final escapade.”

I felt I had to tell someone. Accordingly, I related the whole adventure of my encounter with the ghost in the doorway ... him barring the way. It must have been just ahead of the explosion ... and then nothing.

They both looked incredulous. The story was too far-fetched. There was a prolonged, almost embarrassed silence. "Then again," Jenny ventured. "there is Karrer; you probably don't know. He was going in the door at the other end of the converter shed – we think he was spying on you – and caught the full impact of the blast. They are still picking up the pieces . . . " and her voice trailed away. Not too much grief there, then! More silence for there was nothing much more to say. The two of them, she and the boy friend, quickly said their goodbyes and left me staring into space. I thought, Haber's revenge.

It's hard to believe I was saved by a ghost, Haber's ghost; but what are friends for!

I no longer work in the chemical industry. The money isn't that good.

The Farewell Concert

It's no fun being the manager of a virtuoso. Apart from arranging the season's programme of appearances in various halls around the World, you have to cater for all the foibles, the likes and dislikes of your charge. The hotel has to be right; there has to be a quiet practice room. The transport to the theatre must take them there in good time or they get anxious and fret the time away in the green room. Bertolini is no different to the others I have had to manage over the years; except for the pasta. It has to be just right, otherwise he sulks for the rest of the day.

Bertolini was approaching the end of his career. The endless series of concerts, the meetings with sponsors and fans, the fraught rehearsals with intransigent conductors, the ceaseless travel between gigs were all taking their toll. I could see that retirement was not far from his mind.

This concert was arranged for one of the larger concert halls in London and it had been arranged as part of the PSO touring series with Klaus Degas as conductor. Bertolini was the big attraction though and the main item on the programme with the result that there had been considerable friction between him and Degas. So what was new! It goes with the job and sometimes it lies with me to smooth things between protagonists.

The morning rehearsal with the orchestra went reasonably well in spite of the usual bellowing from the conductor and the missed cues from the orchestra. The Brahms Violin Concerto is not the easiest work to rehearse but the cello section was in good form, which pleased the soloist. However, Degas and Bertolini almost came to blows over the tempo for the slow movement. I must say that it is the soloist's prerogative to choose the speed of his solo. Degas shook his baton at Bertolini; Bertolini shook his Amati violin at Degas and in the end, the rehearsal finished amiably enough without fisticuffs.

On the evening of the concert, Bertolini arrived with his large double case. He always carried a spare instrument in case of breakdown. The practice was the legacy of the occasion when the tailgut of his instrument snapped and he had to borrow one from the orchestra. That breakdown would never happen today with the introduction of metal 'tailguts'. Nevertheless, the ritual continued.

The orchestra was in the process of filing onto the stage and we could hear them warming up as we made our way to the green room. Bertolini was unusually restless as he paced back and forth and brusquely grunted occasionally at a passing acquaintance.

Right on cue, the PSO tuned and got going with a Rossini overture, a strange item for a Brahms concert. It must have been Degas's choice. He never did have much taste. My man squirmed somewhat as he carried his case as always to a table in the wings.

Applause and Degas flustered into the wings to lead the soloist onto the stage. Both had that fake smile typical of the pair, almost like two boxers entering the ring. Concerts can be like that at times and this was one of those times. A pause! The lower strings launched into the beautiful work with the confidence of the professional, a sweeping opening subject in D, gradually developing into a long introduction before Bertolini took up the central role with a sweep of sweetness on the Amati instrument.

There was no hiccup as they moved into the slow adagio movement at Bertolini's tempo. Then the change from F back to D for the final movement.

The applause was ecstatic as Bertolini walked to the wings and carefully placed his instrument back into its case to mop his brow. As his manager, I had to smile encouragingly even though the performance was not all that great; and he knew it. He was certainly getting on in years and was a bit uncertain in the upper register. Yet his magnificent instrument had carried him through the evening with its 350 years of experience. As the ovation continued, I patted his shoulder gently. "They are calling for an encore," I urged. "I know, I know, Frank but I make such ze lousy bog of ze Brahms . . ." and his broken English trailed off with a decided shade of despair. I didn't wish to agree with him and again patted his shoulder to spur him on. In the end he squared his shoulders picked up his instrument and returned to the platform.

A hush descended as he raised the Amati to his shoulder testing its tuning by gently brushing his left fingers over the strings. A brief pause before lifting his bow then sweeping it across all four strings in the magnificent opening spread chords of the piece. I stared in disbelief as I recognised the opening of the magnificent D minor Chaconne of Bach. 'He's not going to play that,' I thought! 'It's at least 15 minutes. It should only be a 3 to 5 minute piece for an encore. The audience is going to get restless.' Yet they didn't.

The music continued effortlessly from its dotted quavers to the super-smooth semis and then into the exciting demi-semis rising to a climax leading suddenly to a more ethereal section. The fast arpeggios sang on through to the original spread chords before serenely gliding into the D major pastoral passage, building up to the return to minor with a gradual and magnificent reminder of the start in great fortissimo chords. I had never once heard Bertolini play with such emotion and as the last single long minim faded to the rafters, there was a stunned hush before rapturous acknowledgement chased him from the stage.

"That was wonderful," I exclaimed, "wonderful!"

He mopped his brow once more and wiped his hands with his handkerchief. Taking a deep breath, he picked up his instrument and returned to the platform once more, he bowed and bowed and bowed. Was there no ending to this evening? He spread his arms wide as though to embrace his audience, his bow in his right hand, his Amati in his left, both trembling with emotion. Then the inconceivable happened. With all the vibration, there was a rattle from the sound post, the instrument's bass-board collapsed and the table of the violin disintegrated with a sharp crack, shards of pine everywhere. At that instant, its soul fled. 350 years had caught up with the instrument and surely the time had come too for the maestro to retire.

Next day, the press really had a spree. Depending on the paper, the headlines varied from

VIOLIN EXPLODES – Russians suspected . . .

To

VALUABLE VIOLIN COLLAPSES AT CONCERT – In last night's concert given by the PSO, a valuable Amati violin disintegrated . . . artist Bertolini devastated . . .

Yes, it was the end of the line for both Bertolini and his instrument. He retired and bought a villa in the South of Italy with the half million pound insurance.

Some years later, I had the occasion to visit Bertolini at his retirement villa. A beaming figure of the man himself met me at the villa gates. "Come in, come in Frank and stay a while. It is good to zee you again after all zis time. It must have been at my last concert; yes, that was ze last time," and he ushered me into a dark shaded cave of a room. Once my eyes had adjusted, one of first things I noticed was an open double-instrument case with just one violin. It looked remarkably like that old Amati, but who am I to judge! I did wonder though . . .

Pétomane

I stared long and hard at the message on my machine. It was from the vicarage; for it was that time of year again – Christmas. I knew it was, for it was an annual invitation to tea. You see, I'm a conjuror, a magician, a prestidigitator, call me what you will. However, I'm not a children's entertainer and the vicar was about to ask me to entertain at the Christmas party as in previous years. Not that I was a great success – not by my standards anyway – for children's magic is a speciality outside my ken and I don't really have their magic-story apparatus.

Not that I mind the vicar. He's an easy-going type – used to keep pigs in his back garden – It's really his overpowering wife I can't stand, all tweed and teeth, (his second wife really). She's the one who got rid of the pigs. Couldn't stand the competition, I expect. To tell the truth, she terrifies me. Still! A summons is a summons and I'll have to go.

Come Thursday, there we were gathered in the large front room at the rectory reserved for such meetings. It was cold, somewhat dusty and there was more than a hint of *eau de pigs.* What's more, my back was playing up again in spite of a double dosage of pregab . . .something-or-other tablets. It was the usual suspects; McCallum with his pipes, Jessie Pinkerton and her two talking dolls, Big Jeannie Cross (Jolly Jeannie) for the games and me, Magic Pete, anything but jolly. For the opposition, we had Mrs Vicar with the Vicar as referee in tow.

I'm not sure why we bothered with such a meeting, for the format was the same as last year – and the year before and the one before that . . . the Vicar would introduce us, Jessie would start; then Jolly Jeannie with some games followed by Magic Me. Hopefully the games would tire the savages before they got to me. McCallum would pipe in a giant Christmas pudding (I don't know why) as the prelude to Santa. "That's settled then," boomed Mrs Vicar and tea was served. I think it was tea.

During tea, I pulled the Vicar aside and explained to him that I was no longer that bright young man full of energy, that I was over seventy and my back ached. "Nonsense, Peter dear," cut in an eves-dropping Mrs Vicar, flashing her teeth; "the little ones adore your show." And that was that. I shuddered, withdrew with aching back and gritted teeth (my teeth.) The Vicar just smiled apologetically and withdrew to join Big McCallum in the corner. He already had his instructions to play quieter this year. "That's no' possible, Mistress. They're meant to be played loud! It scares the Sassenachs, ye ken." Mrs Vicar withdrew with gnashing teeth – a mistress indeed. One up to Big Jock!

Later that night and refortified with more pain killers, I started thinking about a suitable programme for this event. I'll start with the Vanishing Cane and try to avoid a lacerated hand this time, maybe my Milk Jug but not the Squared Circle, such a bother to pack . . . and so I drooled on into the night.

It was only next day that the idea came to me over breakfast. I was in the middle of reading the pamphlet for my pain killers, as you do over breakfast; the various side effects: I seem to have the lot, dizziness, confusion, memory loss, constipation, flatulence, dry mouth; and so it goes on. Yes, I have the lot. I also have an idea for the end of my act; for I was determined that my show would be the highlight of the party.

I put my programme together and jiggled it about a bit, added the Chinese Rings and periodically practised the grand finale until all ran smoothly. It wouldn't, of course, for the unpredictable inevitably arises. That's half the fun in magic - improvisation.

Came the day. I arrived there early to set up and to remind myself of the layout, in particular the fire exits. The others had arrived too and did their preparation avoiding conversation for McCallum had started blowing up his pipes or whatever. Some helpers poked faces round the door and withdrew double-quick.

The kids poured in from the mess hall (I think that describes the room) and slithered along an improvised jelly slide while others simply cavorted noisily here and there. Enter Mrs Vicar and silence. She arranged them into three rows before the makeshift stage and the entertainment programme took off.

The vicar made his customary speech, I think I had heard it before, and Jessie got on with her 'vent' act, a conversation between a naughty boy and his sister. I think that Jessie's act is improving and more convincing. Jolly Jeannie took to the floor for games – pass the parcel, 'In and out the dusty bluebells' and others that were new to me. All that ran off more calories before Mrs Vicar rearranged them into their rows. Now it was my turn with a storm approaching.

A quick check on my props table; all OK. The chair in place; yes. So all was ready. Zip! The cane changed into a silk with no fingers removed; so that was deemed a success. Mild applause. Now the disappearing milk in a newspaper – a few drips but nothing much. On to the next part as the wind gathered. And so on through my programme. Now for the change which I thought required some introduction. "Now, boys and girls, a change to my usual programme. I want you to join me and my penny whistle in the song, Skip to Ma Loo." To my horror, Mrs Vicar stood up to conduct the group – not exactly in my plan. "No, no! It's OK, ma'am." But she insisted.

The kids knew the song and started alright, "Flies in the buttermilk, two by two . . . " and so on to "Skip to ma loo ma darling," or as the little lads sang, "Skip to THE loo . . ." Next verse with much vigorous conducting from the Vicar's wife and the wind continued gathering;

"She's gone again, skip to ma loo," ditto, ditto.

On the last line, I turned and leant on the back of the chair and played the last line thus:

"F a r t fart fart, F a r t , f a r t Faaaaart Faaaaart."

I turned back to a short-lived silence, gaping mouths and two tweedy arms in mid-beat. Then all hell broke loose. Screams of raucous hoots of glee, sniggering and chortling and great hilarity with such a din that McCallum took it as his cue for the pipes. In he marched with pipes raging followed by a giant Christmas pudding and now joined by a troop of the youngsters, round and round the hall. Me? Quick exit stage right.

* * *

In some ways, I miss these Christmas parties. On the other hand, I landed quite a number of proper magic gigs with special requests. But the special request was never repeated.

Jock McCulloch

Maybe it's a getting-old thing, but I recently had a hankering to return to my roots, not all the way, you understand, merely a visit to the backdrop of my early years. From about 5 to 15 years old, I lived in a little village called Rankinston – pronounced 'Ringstn' by the locals. I attended the village Infant School followed by the Junior Secondary before travelling by train each day to Ayr and to Ayr Academy once I had passed the 'Qually'. So it was with some expectation mixed with anticipation that I made the car journey back to Ringstn.

As I drove up the steep hill – I remembered it well – past the junior school, I was surprised at the familiarity of everything in spite of the years. This was my first time since around 1946. There were the houses virtually as I remembered them – Kerse Terrace leading to Littlemill Place, Coyle Crescent and the Avenue. The houses hadn't changed but the infrastructure had. There was now a Co-op, the Mission Hall had been replaced with a Community Hall (I don't know what happened to the missionaries, just that the natives looked pretty smug); there was even a car park. There is no longer a scout hut, the bowling green has been dug up, the New Bar (The Bung, to the locals) has been razed to the ground and the railway station was no more. What was more apparent was that the bustle of the place had gone. It had lost its *raison d'être.*

In former days, Ringstn had a purpose. It was a mining village with several pits in the area. Its people were mining folks with their joys and sorrows, life and death. It was my encounter with the latter that sticks in my mind and it was in the days when there was still a railway chopping the village in two.

It must have been around 1946, just after World War II, when things were still tight including money. Various things were still rationed and travel was thin on the ground. Ringstn had two passenger trains per day really for transport of youngsters to The Academy. That amounted to around 6 children, the others of an age continued at the local school. Occasionally, we had the illustrious company of the local MP, Sawny Sloan on his way to Westminster. My memory of him is as a figure in pin-stripe and bowler with wisps of hair peeping out. An election poster too: **Vote for Sloan – One of your Own.** I had a season ticket that gave me travel to and from school every day. Any extra curricula activity meant I had to make alternative arrangements, usually a combination of train and bus and it is around one of these occasions that my story dwells.

It was getting into late autumn and at school the year was progressing as ever. I had already started a Magic Circle and about half a dozen of us would gather of a lunchtime once a week. Because of this interest, I was invited to perform at our so-called Halloween Ball – it was really a school dance in fancy dress. I had some plastic false teeth in the style of Dracula so that dictated the rest of my costume. Moreover, one Christmas I had acquired a stage make-up box containing all sorts of grease sticks including a luminous variety of a horrible greenish colour. So I was all set.

Come the day, or really the Thursday evening, I donned my costume (essentially black) in the boys' lavi and applied the hideous creamy make-up. Some blacked up eyebrows and the plastic teeth completed the picture. With my stack of tricks in a green portmanteau, I must have looked a treat as I exited the cloakrooms – well not so much a treat, more an indulgence.

Entering the boys' gymnasium in stocking feet – outdoor shoes were not allowed – I was greeted by similarly weird figures in equally grotesque costumes. I waved at one or two I recognised, for I had discarded my spectacles in my haste and my sight was not all that great. I suppose it was an excuse for leering closely at the girl talent. The bouquet of sweaty stockings was unmistakable – this season's perfume.

Thus the evening kicked off. The School Orchestra (well, part of it as it was essentially piano and two violins) tuned up and got things going with a waltz. The boys gathered at one end of the gym (as boys do) and the girls at the other (inevitably). Some ventured into the middle and gradually the whole ghoulish affair started to warm up. I even twirled around with Jean, a witch with white creamy make up who just happened to be in our magic Circle. To help relieve the tedium, I borrowed a violin and took my shot in the 'orchestra'. I remember we played, "Oh my little tangerine," which I later discovered was "Angeline." My additional contribution to the evening was my magic show – disappearing milk from a newspaper, the hanging coins and cut and restored rope. Ye Gods! When I think about it, I'm still doing those tricks today.

The party warmed up and time *'Flew on Angels Wings'* to quote Rabbie. Indeed I lost count of the hour and before I knew it, I had missed the last bus home. That posed a little problem. I couldn't phone home; people didn't have phones in those days, leastways very few did. The lines were reserved for the armed forces and it would be a long time before they became common place. The only thing for it was to find some other way in the general direction of home.

I left the party and legged it quickly to the railway station, a route which incidentally I took every day as part of my school commute. Still wearing my costume and make-up, I made urgent enquiries about trains to Dalmellington; I knew that the line took me to about five miles from my home destination. In answer, the porter replied, "Would that be the ghost train yer after then?" Ha ha, big laugh! "It's over there platform 9 . . . leaving in five minutes . . . and yes, it stops at all stations including Holehouse Junction." He glanced at my student season ticket and nodded me through even though it was well after school hours.

I dashed up platform 9 through the haze of steam with its characteristic odour, opened a compartment door and dropped in. The carriages in those days comprised individual compartments with no joining corridor so you just had to take whatever company was there. That I found out once I'd wiped the steam from my glasses. There was a couple opposite giggling, no doubt when they saw me in full costume and diagonally there was a tipsy guy, *'unco fu and unco happy!'*

With its customary lurch, the train moved off into the night. The dull lighting in the compartment reflected the steam ghosts as they wandered past the closed window. Most of the blinds were down but I had mine raised so that I could gaze into the night. The distant puffing of the engine was accompanied by the slow rhythmic click–click, click-click of the wheels on the rails. I guessed we were racing along at a breakneck 20mph. The background was almost soporific but I daren't doze for fear of missing my stop and I had no desire to continue on to Dalmellington.

The giggling couple left at Dalrymple, the first stop and I was left with my well-oiled companion. Another lurch and we were off again. My worse for wear friend could not take his eyes off me. After some time he ventured, "Are ye no' weel, son?" "No, No! I'm fine." Click- click, click-click. "Ye dinna look fine tae me." "No! I'm alright, fine."

A few clicks further, "Whar are ye gaun, then son?" I looked at him for a time. "I'm just off to Holehouse to haunt a place up that way," I joked. He stared for some time . . . click-click . . . and then, "That's all right, then son. I thoucht ye wisna weel." There endeth the conversation.

What seemed like an eternity, we stopped at Holehouse and I bade my companion goodnight. No reply. He had already fallen asleep. Two other passengers climbed down (the platform is low and requires some agility); they made off towards Patna and I turned to take the line towards home. The little of the way I could see by the single light on the platform which revealed the track and sleepers disappearing into the night. Resolutely I set off by the light of a third of a moon intermittently revealed in a restless sky. It was the sort of sky frequently used when Boris Karloff was abroad.

The sleepers were spaced just right for my pace and I made good progress. Do you find in such a situation that you start counting the paces? I did just that and for a time all I noticed was the echoing clip clop of shoe leather on wooden slabs. Gradually, however, I became aware of other sounds, night sounds, sounds you don't notice during the day because of background noise. The rustle of nearby shrubs mingle with the loftier sighing of their taller neighbours. Occasionally there would be a trickle from a close-by stream or perhaps the bordering seuch and the night was punctuated by the cries of night animals, owls and the like. Just sometimes there was the screech of a kill, enough to turn the blood to ice. All this trespassed on my ears, on my mood, on my anxiety and there were times when I would turn and look back when I imagined I heard a footfall.

After a time, the intermittent moon revealed a glimmer through the bushes to my left. That would be Kerse Loch, a featureless stretch of water; it gave me a landmark to indicate that I was a mere third of the way to my destination and the night darkened as thicker cloud gathered. Still I plodded on.

Certainly I was nearer home but I was also nearer a bridge that I had thus far pushed to the recesses of my mind. That structure was a substantial stone bridge of no guard rails over a sizeable stream whose name escapes me. The name of the bridge I had <u>not</u> forgotten. The locals called it *Jock McCulloch's Loup,* after he who had committed suicide some years previously. I had visited the godforsaken place a few times before, mainly to gather scribes to make crab-apple jelly and I had once taken the backside out my pants sliding down the banking to the stream. All that had been in daylight. Now it was dark, very dark.

Still the rustling of the shrubs and trees dogged my plodding along the permanent way and I could just see the sleepers between the rails leading off into the distance. Closer and closer I came to the bridge, being careful to keep equidistant between the rails. Any occasion in the past I did the same when crossing this bridge for I had a horror of stepping over the edge. Such is the fancy of the imagination.

There was the bridge. I could sense it before me, that was all. No other indication! No ghost! Now the hollow sound symptomatic of the structure itself and I was over in a trice to continue my journey. Then in a thoughtless moment I looked back. There following me was a ghostly figure – it must have been Jock McCulloch – and in terror I turned completely to face the apparition. Just at that moment, the clouds parted and the moon shone fully on my person, on me in my full party rigout, on my green face. The bodach hesitated, I could sense a silent scream and Jock McCulloch was gone in an instant.

In something of a daze and fear and trembling, I continued my journey home in double quick time. It was only afterwards that I thought . . . that must have been the first record of a ghost being frightened by a ghost, even if only a pretend ghost.

What Sound?

… it must be the sound of silence

I suppose I was in at the beginning. Let me explain.

By trade (or profession) I am an acoustic engineer, whatever that means. To me it means that I analyse sounds. I try to find their sources and their targets. I try to find what causes sounds and how they can be modified. Or perhaps I try to characterise them or even reproduce them. This doesn't just apply to melodious sounds but to rogue ones that might be classified as noise. It is all part of life and living, for where would we be without sound. Some would say *deaf* for this is what we imagine it to be. But only those deaf from birth find it difficult to conceptualize sound – or so we assume. Perhaps they have their own world of sound. Alternatively, take Beethoven (the Ludwig van variety) who only started to go deaf in his early twenties and was completely deaf by his mid forties; he could hear the musical sounds in his head although latterly this was impaired by tinnitus. Perhaps we all have our own little world of sound or fantasized sound. I know that when learning to play the violin as a youngster, I imagined the sounds produced were those of a virtuoso – all in the head, you see, judging by the listeners' reaction. You can tell just by the pained facial expression of the audience.

Of course as an acoustic engineer, I was initially involved in the design of hearing aids, so naturally I got to know a number of hearing-impaired people and to sympathise with them to a large extent. This drew me into a desire to explore further this sphere of science and accordingly I pursued research in the subject. Even though I say it myself (no one else will otherwise) I became something of an expert in audiology. What I found disturbing at the time was the hearing ability of youngsters, what with the noisy world we were all living in. Young people have a wide range of sound wavelength sensitivity and it bothers me to realise that they spend long periods in very loud surroundings whether that be at a pop concert or in their car with the radio turned up full blast. I can recall a summer vacation job I had as a student. It was in the brick industry and on occasions I had to work at 'lifting off', that is, lifting 'green' brick from a die-stamping machine onto a bogie. The machinery dated back to Victorian times and operated at a high level of noise so much so that conversation was impossible. After a shift (something like 10 hours) all I could hear in my mind was the racket of heavy machinery, little else, all night long. I can still feel the effects today with somewhat dull hearing.

Loss of hearing is also a hazard for professional musicians playing in a large orchestra. They may be playing or rehearsing for prolonged periods in the heart of a high level intensity sound zone. This can be particularly stressful if you happen to be a string player placed in front of the brass section – I know; I've been there. Health and Safety stepped in and now insist that some sort of barrier – such as a Perspex sheet - be placed in front of the brass section. Some strings insist they can still see them and suggest something more substantial and decidedly opaque!

Enough of that blethering on! Next thing you know I'll be preaching about the downgrading of music in schools' curricula. My research area is studying abnormalities in acoustics which of course includes hearing. Odd acoustical phenomena are reported to me or sometimes proactively collected by me and such pursuit takes me all over the world. The most recent has taken me to, of all places, the Dutch East Indies and in particular, a rural area of the Island of Borneo.

Flying on my way there, I was given the low-down on the problem by my travelling companion, Dr Julie Hendersen who was the medical side of the team. It seems that a local group of Dayak had developed some sort of hearing problem over quite a short period. It was now our task to characterise the problem and if possible find its cause and cure, no easy task for our short three-month stay there. As it happened, three months was more than enough, what with the rain.

We landed at Palembang in south Sumatra before changing to a local plane service for Kota. After a brief pause there, we completed our journey in teeming rain by Landrover to a tiny Dayak village about two hours inland, all laid on by our Malaysian hosts. I suppose this is what is called the Rain Forest; it certainly lived up to its name.

At the village destination, they had managed to tow a series of caravans for accommodation and two larger ones to act as laboratories. These were somewhat basic but they would do the job. By nightfall, we had settled in and eaten – a vegetable curry dish. For this I was grateful. Perhaps I would have been suspicious had there been meat involved for I had heard that cannibalism was rife in the area; hence my apprehension.

Tomorrow, we would get down to the business of commissioning the laboratories.

The next day, it was to hell with the laboratories. Lets get back to Kota and buy some wellies. Mine were green and the Doc's yellow. I had wanted tartan ones (just to be different) but it was not to be . . . great disappointment. Anyway, back to the camp with the wellies and some waterproof coats which were little more than polythene bags with arms!

Over the following few days, we spent the time getting everything organised and in order. One of the labs. was essentially for acoustic equipment; the other was the medical centre and we began interviewing the local Dayaks one by one. We recorded as far as we could the time each one started going dull of hearing. Not knowing the local dialect or indeed the general language, we relied on a Malaysian interpreter by name, Tunku. It seemed a peculiar language sound-wise for it sounded just like a lot of vowels strung together, you could say almost like Glasgow on a Saturday night. It seemed too that Tunku was having difficulty with the language.

I did the usual tests with a controlled sound source, to determine the range of damage. Initially, I found the results unusual. Not only was there damage to the high frequencies but also to the low ones. In other words, this group of Dayaks could only detect the middle frequency range. It's usually the upper frequencies which go first . . . most disturbing. Why?

Moreover, Julie found that essentially the Dayak's diet was vegetarian, most unusual for this part of the island. We jumped to the conclusion that there was something vital missing from the diet. Either that, or part of the diet was contributing to the hearing problem. This seemed to be confirmed when we found that the villagers had only recently changed to this vegetarianism. So the next question was; what made them change?

We looked long and hard at the Dayak's food menu. We tried asking them why they had changed. In the end, the answer was obvious and we had approached the problem from the wrong end. The villagers had started to go seriously deaf first and then found that they could no longer hunt successfully. They made too much noise without realising. So the cause of the hearing loss had nothing to do with the diet. There must be some other answer, a virus or some sort of bug. This meant some kind of post mortem appraisal. We were soon to find out that this was not possible. It was against the ethics of the Dayaks to invade the body of the dead in such a manner.

"I think our job here is finished, Julie." She agreed: "We'll just have to take our findings here and publish what we can."

Thus finished our research into this peculiar phenomenon and our visit, our rather wet visit to Borneo.

***

Our findings were duly written up and published and our search for unusual acoustic and audiological events went on. It wasn't long after the publication that similar observations came in from all over the world. There didn't seem to be a common denominator. There was no overwhelming source of noise or music or even rain. The living styles were numerous. The race types were various. The environment and climate assorted. This was a problem and was turning into an epidemic, indeed into a pandemic – and a serious one too.

The next 'happening' we decided to investigate was in Finland. I understood that Julie's background was Scandinavian so it seemed appropriate. Besides she might have useful knowledge of the area. We were destined for a village near Kotka just north of Helsinki. We arrived there on the Friday and as always, we were treated like royalty. Just as before, the locals seemed to have been affected in a similar way to the Malaysian victims. Their speech was slurred and seemed to be short of consonants but there was no leaning towards vegetarianism. A common factor was water. We found ourselves in the midst of vast area of lakes but thankfully not rain, leastways not that day.

As guests, we were invited to the Saturday evening village celebrations, dining and entertainment – lots of folk dances to some peculiar music with lots of rhythm. What I found really strange was the programme item given by the local choir. They sang an item with no discernable words and all approximately on one note. I say approximately for the resultant effect was a sort of flat vibrato like a soprano choir boy sound. Sibelius would be surprised, I fancy; yet his Valse Triste was no sadder than that monotone. I could only put it down to their hearing problem.

After careful examination of all the circumstances, we could find little in common with the Malaysian group. We need to have a brain storming session and recruited some of the expertise from Helsinki Aalto University. Kaisa Balliu arrived on site the following day about 2.00pm and soon made herself known; for she was, shall we say, rather tall and imposing. Following soon after was Asko Kostiainen, the complete antithesis, for his 5ft 1in made him seem timid, a completely wrong analysis for he was a real livewire.

We gathered in a room, part of the village hall, the four of us around a large table. I outlined what we had already done at the two sites visited so far, and what little we had found – the retained hearing, a narrow band around 400 to 500Hz – the effect on speech making it sound featureless – our wild goose chase trying to link vegetarianism with the hearing phenomenon – the discovery that this hearing loss was occurring at sites globally and not just to individuals but to localised groups. Not much to go on to date – quite a perplexing situation. I did mention the village concert more out of interest rather than significance.

As always at the beginning of a research project, we were floundering around trying different avenues and rejecting the unfruitful ones. I am rather suspicious of that so-called research which starts at the end and then tries to fit the information and statistics to that end; there is confusion of *cause* and *effect.* Even Avogadro was uneasy about his Hypothesis.

We sat round looking at each other. "So where do we go from here?" I asked without too much hope. "Any ideas spring to mind?" Kaisa was the first to propose a possible avenue. "Let's get a global map and pin point these occurrences. It might tell us something." Noted.

Asko seemed interested in the efforts of the choir. "I wonder if they hear something that we don't? I'll see what response I can get from the choir members although I must say that I have difficulty interpreting their dialect."

"It's not their dialect. It's the distortion from the hearing problem." We had learnt this through our experiences here and in Borneo. No doubt we'll come across it again before we're finished.

Asko seemed taken aback by this correction. Maybe his students seldom contradicted him. "We've come across this before, you see. It was the same in Borneo." That seemed to mollify him somewhat. I just hoped we could work together as a team rather than take umbrage at every turn.

Julie Hendersen came in at this point with her medical findings. "The various people I've examined seemed quite normal apart from the hearing problem. There is the usual spread of common colds but no abnormal temperatures and the customary scatter of blood pressure readings according to the age group." She paused at this point, gave a nervous little cough and announced: " Of course it would be useful if we could examine the ear internally - perhaps in a post-mortem - if someone would oblige . . . and die!" That suggestion was left hanging for the moment. I did make a mental note however.

"I'll borrow an oscilloscope from the University to try and recognise any abnormal sound effects locally," I suggested and the other three nodded in agreement. "Meantime, we'll pursue the various avenues we've already recognised: Julie, the medical aspects and I'll enquire about the possibility of your sitting in on any pending post –mortems - Kaisa, the map thing - Asco the choir sound analysis and I'll have a look at any local sound anomalies."

There was no problem with borrowing sound equipment; the Aalto University was only too happy to be associated with our project. I duly set up the oscilloscope and made several attempts to try and detect any anomalies in the local sound spectrum. It was certainly easier working here compared to Borneo what with the technical facilities available locally.

I convened another meeting of the group of four for a week hence simply to update each other regarding any sort of progress. I know it was rather soon to expect any progress, but there might be something significant which would change the direction of our research.

Somehow I had a feeling of uneasiness. Where would it all end! It could have been my imagination but I felt that my tinnitus was getting louder. You know how it is, if someone starts discussing bedbugs you start scratching, not that I discuss bedbugs all that often.

As before, we gathered around the table in the hall. I started the proceedings. "Well, I've had nothing but cooperation so far. The locals have been most friendly and are eager to find out what the problem is and what can be done to help. I think they've recognised that there is a problem – that's half the battle. As far as the sound wave profile is concerned, the overall picture is normal – so a bit negative there." The others were a bit restive – I feel that they were anxious to get on with their side of things rather than blether on in a fruitless meeting. Nevertheless, I felt that this communications aspect was vital to our progress. Who knows! Perhaps we were barking up the wrong tree and once you get deeply into an avenue of research, the more reluctant you are to abandon it. Let's press on and not fritter time away by arguing the toss.

Julie was next. "I've made a routine medical examination of the various villagers and it's the same story as before. Just the usual sniffs, occasional coughs, a bit of toothache here and there and the usual aches of old age with the elderly. No post mortem as yet but I did find something significant. The problems started around three years ago and since then there have been 5 births in the village. Of the eldest two at around three years old, they seem to have the same hearing characteristics. Their baby-talk is the same monotone as the adults. At first I thought this was because they were learning from their parents. However I've found that the deficiency is inherent in the youngsters. It's a genetic thing."

There was a stunned silence all round. Whatever the cause, it had affected the genes of the victims. Was this a chemical thing, or perhaps radio active based? Or even some other kind of radiation, even sound waves? The mind boggles. Other questions arise – where is the source? – what is the source? – who is the source? We'll hear the reports from the other two and then decide where we go from here.

Asko seemed anxious to have his say next. Perhaps he had made some progress or significant discovery and he wished to reveal it dramatically. I couldn't be more wrong. "I've had an in-depth discussion with members of the choir and I'm afraid they couldn't throw any light on their strange performance. They were just as puzzled and realised that something was wrong. They just couldn't nail it down. They could only sing what they could hear and that was it. They did pinpoint something peculiar – not really relevant to the singing. All bird life had disappeared from the area.

"Perhaps it's not irrelevant," I ventured. "but it did happen around the same time." I looked around at the others. "Perhaps birds need to hear to hunt - just like those villagers in Borneo - if they can't hunt they starve. Or perhaps they need to hear to sing and hence to mate. This is turning into a case of sound vanishing altogether from this region."

"Kaisa, what have you got for us?" She looked at us all before producing a projection map of the World. "I have marked the various areas where this same phenomenon has been found. There is no straight relationship as far as I could see but this isn't surprising for this map is a planar projection of a sphere. If there is a straight line link, it would appear as a smooth curve. Now I have plotted this location in New South Wales, this one in North Island New Zealand, here in Vietnam, Labrador, Honduras and of course, Finland and Borneo. You can see that there seems to be a smooth curve but it does fall away towards Honduras. What do we deduce from that?"

We looked around at one another. "We'll wait for reports of further sightings before hasty conclusions," I suggested, "and see if this observation is significant. It is surprising certainly. We don't know if this could be some sort of atmospheric contamination drifting along this path . . . "

"I've looked at that possibility," interrupted Kaisa "but the routes of the normal wind currents and even those in the stratosphere are not continuous. But of course we don't know what poisons, or the like, various regimes are pumping into our atmosphere . . . " and at this her voice trailed away.

Just then, someone's mobile went off. It was Kaisa's. After a brief conversation, she turned to us. "That's a colleague of mine who has been modelling these locations using a computer programme. He has come up with an interesting 3D image of these sites on a globe of the World representation. I think we should see this."

On the way back to the university, Kaisa was clearly excited. "The 3D computer image appears to show a distinct hoop around the

Earth," she revealed. "No doubt the aspect of this will give us a clue regarding its origin."

Right enough, it was soon apparent when we arrived in the computing section and saw the graphic that some outside agency had marked the World with a line going all the way round. A few more reported events had been added to the data and backed up the hoop picture. It did not divide the Earth exactly into two; it merely sliced through to give two uneven parts of a sphere (if you can think of Earth as a sphere.)

"So! What do you think? An external source of radiation of some sort – from outer space!!! – but what sort of radiation? It can't be cosmic rays as such. They are certainly high energy particles but they just produce secondary radiations. It must be some other sort of 'cosmic' radiation." So ended my dissertation on rays. I thought the group were about to give me the slow hand-clap, so I continued; "Any idea of the source?"

One of the computer group ventured; "Not unless we know the exact time of the happening." I like that – The Happening. He continued; "It's possible that such an energy source would cause ionization in the upper atmosphere. I am sure there are groups monitoring such ionization – they keep telling us what greenhouse gases do to the ozone layer." About three years ago? I don't remember any particular outcry then. It's worth following up, though.

So back to our foursome conference.

Well, guys," I began. "This thing is turning out to be something bigger than we can handle." I could see Asko squirming. He could see the kudos for the work slipping away. I continued; "We need to get this into print pronto and preferably in a scientific publication."

"That's going to take us forever ... or months anyway," he interrupted. "The situation could have advanced a lot in months!"

There was a jumble of voices with all four of us speaking at once. "All right, all right! But it's important that we explore some other avenues," I suggested. "The real priority is to identify the cause and also the source of the cause." Agreement all round. "Without knowing what we are looking for, we need to determine whether or not this is man-made and therefore we need to find out if there are any projects on the go within the field of acoustics. These are likely to be highly secret and therefore government led. Are any of you aware of anything like this?"

Blank looks all round. "Lets start with a literature search," suggested Kaisa. "We could farm this out to our students as a project." Nods confirmed the idea.

"Why not approach government sources to find if they have any intelligence along this line?" Julie suggested. There were doubtful faces. There was always a reluctance to involve governments in any project, for there was always the additional factor of politics.

"Listen, guys. Somehow I feel that we don't have much time. We have to pursue all and every angle. Julie, you and I will try to penetrate the Ivory Castle of Whitehall. The other two can see what they can do with their government ... " " the Eduskunta," interjected Asko, "... while the literature search goes on. Asko! Can you see if you can find out anything more about disruption to the ozone layer. It may pinpoint more exactly the happening of three years ago."

***

"Hullo! My name's Agnew, Dr Giles Agnew." I held out my hand to the young man before me. "You must be my MP," I suggested.

"Yes, Tom Sloan. What is the problem, Dr Agnew?" No wasted time with idle chat, then!

I explained the work our group had been engaged in and how we were seeking certain information which might be classified. He hesitated somewhat when I mentioned things from outer space and I think he saw our problem trying to identify if it was all a man-made hazard. "I really need to speak to someone from the Home Office - really someone with access to intelligence regarding such research. I don't need any detail. I'm just trying to rule out certain possibilities."

Sloan looked dubious. I pushed on. "Look! This is very important and indeed we need to move quickly on this. Any delay risks further occurrences and I think this could easily become global - indeed, it's already global."

"Leave this with me. I'll see what I can do." With that, Sloan closed the interview and I went back home with a degree of frustration recognising that it would be some time before I saw any results.

I was wrong. Apparently those in higher places had heard of me and my work; for a few days later, I had a phone call summoning me to SIS at Vauxhall Cross. I duly packed my overnight bag and scrambled for the next train South with my lap-top and grip.

I signed in at my usual doss house and made my way to my pending meeting. Arriving there, I was directed to the reception desk by the flunky at the door. I looked around at my surroundings, the marble walls – I think it was real marble – and the ornate ceilings. No doubt I looked like the typical country yokel visiting the Big Smoke for the first time. The impression I got was of one vast public toilet - of the posher sort, of course.

The receptionist looked up as I approached. "Yes?" disapprovingly. A black look from a seated figure in black. "Doctor Agnew! I have an appointment, I believe."

She consulted her desk diary and spoke into her intercom. "Yes, he's here now . . . at the front desk." She directed me to one of the over-comfy chairs. "You'll be collected shortly," and with that she continued with whatever it was she was doing, not the traditional nail polishing.

After a short wait, I was duly 'collected' by a young casually dressed youngster. "Dr Agnew? This way please." He led the way through various corridors of closed doors and dismal paintings, perhaps portraits of former spies. I tried to see if he had a shoulder holster with the usual Beretta. We entered an outer office with its quota of clerical staff and through to a quiet office with superannuated furniture and a near-superannuated figure behind a desk.

"Please sit down, Dr Agnew. If you don't mind, my assistant will sit in too."

No names, you'll notice. Canny folk these spies!

I opened up my lap-top and began my dissertation. The unusual form of deafness . . . the global spread of the affliction . . . the normal health of the victims . . . the global distribution to form a symmetrical hoop. "I've put all this on this stick for you to examine at your leisure," I finished. "The sort of information I'm looking for - Could this be man made? Once we know the cause, we can tackle the remedy."

The Boss nodded sagely. I only hope he really did understand the seriousness of the situation. To a large extent we depended on his intelligence sources to narrow our search. Did he know of any foreign research - Russian or US - which entailed sound wave experiments? If all this fails and we preclude such research then we have to look at extra-terrestrial sources. Perhaps I would have had more response if I had said ALIENS. I deliberately didn't in case they labelled me as just another crackpot.

"I'll look into this with the urgency you seem to wish, Dr Agnew and let you know the outcome," the Boss said indicating that the session was over. I stood, thanked him and handed over the memory stick. With a brief goodbye the assistant led me back through the corridors without a word. At the exit, he merely nodded and I was out into Vauxhall once again.

As I strolled back to my hotel window shopping as I went, I took to looking in the reflections to see if I was being followed, typical spy stuff. It was all just a game, like me making a mental note of the room number, 37 and 37a, and the label on the door, Home Security. I immediately thought of Burglar Alarms Ltd - I don't think it was that. I had to have my little joke. In addition, when the Boss was looking at the video of the spinning Earth with hoop, I took his photo. So much for their security!

Back at the hotel, I arranged a conference call with the other three for 2.00pm and left for a stroll around the sights. However, I took the precaution of replacing the memory card in my laptop with a duplicate presentation card. I must be getting paranoid for I used the old James Bond trick of a hair stuck across the jamb of the door as I left the room.

On returning I set up the conference call. The hair was still in place – so much for my James-Bond distrust theories.

Via the conference, I brought the other three up to date with my activities and my opinion on the likelihood of getting any action out of the powers that be. The most interesting piece of information from the others came from Kaisa. She had been in contact with the operators of the Hadron Particle Accelerator scientists in Geneva only to discover that, about three years ago, their accelerator had been out of commission for long periods. Nonetheless, there had been some unusual activity for two periods during that time. She made a note of the relevant dates and carried these through to further enquiries at Jodrell Bank Observatory via Manchester University. Apparently on those dates, there had been unusual activity in the Andromeda Galaxy about two and a half million light years away, give or take a yard or two. Two of its smaller stars had exploded because of their proximity to each other and the resulting radiation was now reaching Earth at intervals. The nature of the radiation was unknown, but its results I think we realize. However there is another possibility from outer space. In the same galaxy, a known black hole has swallowed up a large planet with the result that there is a stream of radiation from that source. It's also an unknown type, perhaps black hole indigestion.

All we can do now is to try and map the occurrences and identify the nature of these radiations. Until we know that we cannot give any guidance for a suitable protection. There is quite a bit of turmoil out there in space; then again I understand that this happens frequently.

At that stage, there was a break in communication, not unusual with these conferences. I decided just to email the others for we had finished business.

For the next few weeks we continued our searches without any progress. I thought I would try to prod the SIS to find out whether their side of things had made any progress for I was beginning to feel that they had taken me as some sort of crank. Firstly, I prepared a press statement outlining what we had found so far and sent a copy to the other three. I then printed out a paper copy in preparation for sending to the office in Vauxhall. My covering letter stated that I thought the general public should be made aware of the situation – hence the statement to the press. I also stated my disappointment at the lack of information regarding their progress on the intelligence side. I addressed the envelope to Room 37a of their offices.

I received a quick response by email to the effect that such a document sent to the press would initiate public panic adding that any such press release would have a D-notice placed on it. In addition, there had been no intelligence identifying any such relevant international research.

Anyway, they were too late. There was another hoop of occurrences around the globe and this time it was international news. This time the hoop described a path through central USA affecting cities such as Atlanta, Dallas and Long beach. The first thought was that Russia was the culprit until the UK put them wise to our observations elsewhere. Besides, the hoop ran through part of Southern Africa and was followed by another cutting through Kazakhstan as well as central Europe.

Needless to say, SIS got hold of me pretty quickly after that to find out what further information I had on the phenomena. To a large extent though, we were all in the dark and the whole matter was taken out of my hands. Our little group of four was subsumed into a larger consortium which seemed to do little but have meetings. We were consulted little on the matter and in the end I went my own way as did Julie and Kaisa. I don't know what happened to Asko and perhaps he continued within the consortium; for I heard nothing about him or from him thereafter.

***

About three years have gone by since those heady days and I have heard nothing from the group – literally, for now I am completely deaf. I now commit all my comments to paper. As for the past record, this has been downloaded to paper too.

A lot has happened over this past period. To begin with, the hearing loss seemed to make little difference to the everyday operation of society. After all, it had always been with us through the ages. Then again, it hadn't affected so many before. As it became more widespread, it started to encroach into everyday life. I was attending a football match on one occasion when the affliction suddenly affected the whole crowd; that is when I was knocked back. The outcome on the general assembly was delayed until the crowd noticed that it could no longer hear itself cheer or offer advice to the referee. Indeed, the referee could no longer hear his whistle despite banging it against his hand several times. Soon the game turned chaotic and the whole thing was abandoned. It may seem trifling to some but to others, it was their whole *raison d'être.* A visit to the pub was meaningless without the banter. Office work came to a standstill.

This same radiation effect had struck virtually the complete global population. It damaged satellite operation and all types of radio waves were ineffective. The World was cut off from itself.

Parliament closed for there was no one to listen (no change there then); indeed government of all kinds disintegrated and all services petered out. Shops were looted and everyone ran amok. Law and order didn't exist. Civilization ceased.

After the initial upheaval there was a pause in activity. No one seemed to know what to do next, or if they did, they couldn't communicate it to others. As far as I understand, people seemed to be ending everything with suicide, but it was difficult to convey such information if it were true. There were no newspapers. Delivery of goods particularly food was non-existent. No doubt there were piles of food somewhere in great rotting piles – but where?

The tinnitus hissing in my head had taken a different profile; for now it alternated with a roaring of motorbikes – hiss, burr, hiss, burr – on and on. Normally I can thrust the hissing into the background, simply ignore it; but no longer. It was driving me mad.

I had had enough. I was getting out. There was no transport and petrol had run out long since. I still had some in my car hidden away in my garage and I reckoned it was enough to get me to my holiday cottage. Well, it wasn't really a cottage, more a shepherd's bothy. This was set at the end of a track in the depths of Argyll. It was quite a cosy little place protected from westerlies by a bolt of pines. Mind you, I had only used it in summer.

I quickly exited my flat and made for my lock-up. There was chaos everywhere and the stench of death in the air. The tinnitus in my head soared with my pulse. All around was deserted. No mobs. No madmen. No nothing. With great speed (for me) I opened up the garage, climbed in the car and got out of there dodging round the debris lying everywhere. In no time I was away from it all and heading on a deserted road north.

I am now in my less-than-cosy mountain bothy sprawled on an easy chair that has seen better days. My food supplies are pretty basic – meal, flour, a selection of unappetising tins and a tub of butter. Winter is closing in fast although I have been hard at work sawing up some windfalls from the sheltering pines. Already there is a little flurry of snow and the surroundings feel decidedly colder. I wonder if I shall see the spring? There is always my paracetamol!

This account or history or whatever you want to call it resides in a little leather case next to the remains. Some day, perhaps, it will be found by a survivor; for there are survivors who manage to adapt to a soundless world, to a much poorer world. There may even come a time when sound and all its delights return!

The bothy is dripping, its window frames crooked and glass cracked. The little leather case is now green with mould. Already there is a swallow building a nest in the eaves. Listen carefully (if you can hear) and you will make out its chirping – that's the sound of hope! Don't they migrate from Africa?

LETTERS FROM A STRANGER

It's odd how things happen. The first communication was by e-mail; and it was a strange one. Usually my computer weeds out unidentified material but this one sneaked through somehow. It opened to reveal the image of a playing card, simply the ace of spades, and I didn't think it singular initially, for I do receive adverts from various magic companies trying to sell their wares. Just the same, the plain unadorned card with no accompanying explanation was slightly disturbing.

I thought no more about it until later that week, the first letter arrived by conventional post. Usually when I get mail, I try to guess who sent it, not from the frank stamp (for it tells you nothing these days) but from the manner of address. "Hand addressed" are usually personal and I seldom get these unless it is a birthday card or perhaps a Christmas one. On the other hand, if it is formally typed with "Mr A . . . " it is business. If it is addressed "to the householder" they are circulars destined for recycle - you know the sort of thing. This envelope was addressed as personal so I opened it and out dropped a playing card, the 2 of spades. How bizarre!

There was nothing unusual about the card, just a plain bridge-size playing card. I stared at it lying there on the hall table. It stared back. I suppose it was unusual in that it was bridge-size for I use the slightly larger poker-size cards. That was all. No covering note or greeting or advert; just a plain ordinary playing card with the reverse side showing it was manufactured by Piatnik.

The following morning, the same thing happened but with the 3 of spades this time; and the next morning, and the next. The following day too, which was unusual; for it was a Sunday and post never comes on a Sunday. That was when I noticed for the first time that the envelope had no stamp. How did I miss that? Quite simply because the others did have stamps but this one must have been hand delivered. So, someone had sneaked the envelope through my letterbox.

This continued for several weeks from late autumn into the approach of winter and I accumulated quite a collection. I examined the back of one of the cards essentially to see if they were marked. They had some sort of shady background depicting two figures, an unfamiliar design for Piatnik. So what! There are numerous card-back designs on the market. Indeed some people collect them for fun, sort of like collecting stamps or even parking tickets.

I boxed the cards and fanned them. By now I had almost the full pack of these quite good quality pasteboards. I riffled them with my thumb, turned them over and riffled them again. This time I did notice that picture on the back seemed to move, a sure sign of a marked deck. 'I'll arrange them in pack order and tried another riffle to see if I could decipher the marking code', I thought. The image on the card back moved like some primitive film show. One figure had a sword and was in the act of beheading the other when the action stopped in mid-air. The pack, of course was as yet incomplete.

Imagine my horror with thoughts of what was to follow. I dreaded the arrival of the next card, but come it did and I added it to the pack. The sword moved ever closer to the neck.

The nights were disturbed with restless sleep. I would start with apprehension at every little night sound, a drip of toilet water, the creak of a timber, the rattle of an ill-fitting window frame. I would twist and turn and occasionally got up to walk around the chilly bedroom only to get cold feet (literally), keeping me awake for the rest of the night.

It had been snowing and surely this would show the footprints of the culprit. I waited all alert for the next card; and waited; and waited. Whoever it was took advantage of my toilet break for the next delivery. I opened my front door but any give away footprints were obliterated by the confusion of passing traffic, in particular wee Charlie's tracks. The eight-year-old from next door had been building a snowman in my front garden, just to cheer me up by his way of it.

The latest card, the king of diamonds, virtually completed my pack. The only card missing was the ill-famed ace of spades. That was the first card and it had arrived by email. By now, the sword had almost completed its mission. Tomorrow's delivery would be final.

The night was long and restless. Dark shadows fleeted across my mind as I tossed and turned. I thought I could hear voices murmur and the sough of the wind added to the darkness. To add to all that, my feet were freezing.

Next morning, this wet rag dragged himself downstairs, filled the kettle and sat down to breakfast, such as it was. Halfway through, the doorbell rang. I choked on my Shreddies and stumbled to the door. With trepidation I threw open the door with seemingly no one there till I looked down. There was wee Charlie from next door. "Hey mister! That man chopped the heid aff yer snowman wi' his stick;" and he pointed to a vague figure hurrying over the near horizon.

I burst into a great roar of laughter, more in relief than anything. A scared Charlie scurried away to his own garden in double quick time. I think he was somewhat startled. "It's alright, Charlie. We'll mend it together." He still seemed uncertain.

Closing the door, I noticed the new envelope on the doormat. I wasn't surprised. I opened it and surprise, surprise, it was the ace of spades. I turned it over; there was a picture of a headless . . . snowman.

From Feet to Conservation!

Canna is a bonny wee island in the Little Minch and today it is at its best with sunshine and a kind breeze. There are many gentle walks inviting the visitor (that's me) to explore. I have ventured down a faint path to a bank of sand and listened to the little waves sliding up the shore and back, lisping all the way (to quote MacCaig.) There were shells on the beach which draped itself from the ruined castle-come-prison to a seemingly precarious escarpment.

Time to give Feet a rest from this heat! Off with the boots and woolly socks! I sit on a rock and look down at corpse-white Feet dangling in glassy water. Poor Feet! No one finds you attractive – let's face it, you're downright ugly. No one has anything good to say apropos Feet. Even our language derides you – people crushed underfoot. . . under the heel of . . . given the boot . . . Oh, my dogs . . . flatfooted . . . two left feet. Little minnows come and nibble cheese pizzas; the waves chuckle at the thought.

After all these years (I'm just over 30), you have held me aloft, carried me along usually without complaint. There is the occasional ingrown toenail, perhaps a corn or a skinned heel and there was that time I had *plantar fasciitis*; but over the years you have served me well. You would think that being over 30 things would start to get better, to ease off. Not a bit of it! Let's accept that as I get on a bit, I put on a bit – I refer to weight. And it all presses down on my plates, a term used when I can't face up to the word feet. You are now carrying 2 stone more than you should. The only occasion when feet can be cute is before you can walk; yes! babies' tootsies.

Sometimes Feet would look at cousins, Hands with something akin to envy. Hands can be beautiful, elegant, authoritative, even rude. A single finger can point the way, can point accusingly, can point aggressively. It can pick a nose or howk wax from an ear. It can retrieve the smallest of coins from a Highlander's sporran. Is there no end to its versatility! Hand's palm is equally versatile. It can be begging . . . aggressive with a slap . . . mercenary with a back-hander. It can even do a foot's job, if you can stand on your hands – I haven't tried recently.

There are occasions when Hand can be rude; it can give you the push. Even a single finger can be rude, depending on your choice. It can even be cute when it's a thumb that's being sucked. When a finger and thumb are combined, things are hunky-dory; but two fingers are very rude. Three fingers are used by Boy Scouts when saluting or rubbing 2 sticks together. Four fingers when your best friend is buying the next round, or he will be if he ever does; or a farewell wave with five fingers if he doesn't, combined with the aforementioned two.

Hands can do so many things I can't do – it's Feet speaking. My cousins can take a chalk and create a masterpiece, or some oily paint, even gouache not to mention watery pigments and turn them into a meaningful image. A single finger – or more – can pluck a string and make a soul weep, as clarsachs do. Fingers press keys on a wistful oboe . . . a playful flute . . . a melancholy clarinet . . . a jokey bassoon. It can translate black dots to sublime sounds from early Frescobaldi through joyful Haydn to romantic Rachmaninoff – the heaven is filled with crochets and quavers while semibreves hover and demisemiquavers rain to earth, the great joy of music. To boss all, the conductor waves his hands about in front of an orchestra with meaningless gestures, so they think. He thinks differently and justifies the gestures as his/her interpretation. Come to think, you can conduct with feet. Many's the time, sitting with feet up listening to music, I've conducted with a foot.

Hands get all the fun too . . . the fond caress . . . the gentle stroke . . . the tender massage. But don't the Chinese massage backs by standing on them, kneading? So Feet, have your fun too! Indeed, in their own dimension, Feet may overcome their own shortcomings; conduct music . . . Chinese massage. It is all a matter of adaption, perhaps retraining. I continually admire those artists who persevere in expressing their talents after losing the use of their hands, the Mouth and Foot Painting Artists. So, get on your feet, Feet and get cracking – you can do it!

"Hoy there Kenny." It was Charley Munroe who interrupted my dwam. "I hear you are off to Inverness tomorrow."

"Aye, that's right enough. That's when I give my paper to the Conference on Conservation and I should say that I'm not all that confident. I have all the material prepared and typed. It's the presentation I'm not so happy about. I haven't done this sort of thing before."

"Nothing to it!" Charley exclaimed. "Just read it straight from your notes. Just a wee hint, though. It's a good idea to stand at the beginning and stare at the audience – a bit of a pause at the beginning. That gets their attention."

With that bit of wisdom, I returned to my let cottage to prepare for my journey.

Next day, the ferry took me to Mallaig on the mainland where a short walk took me to the railway station. There I joined the Hogwarts Express sighing at the platform. It was almost as though it had been impatiently waiting for me, as of course it had.

With a final protracted sigh, the Express took off on its roaming through the hills and glens of Western Scotland, a sedate journey to be sure. No-one seemed to mind the pace. The leisurely click from the track with an occasional toot and it seemed no time till we were rolling over the Glenfinnan viaduct, curving back to look at itself, as it does. In no time the train was running alongside Loch Eil and Corpach into the town of Fort William.

The 2-hour bus journey from Fort William to Inverness was a daydream. Various landmarks passed through the haze, Fort Augustus then Drumnadrochit and there I was in the middle of the town not far from the Ness Hotel, a rather imposing building from the Victorian era. That was to be my accommodation and the centre for the conference.

There was a reception desk inside the entrance with tweedie and bearded folks (not necessarily both) milling around. I duly signed in and received a wad of papers with programme, information about eating and various other bits of essentially publicity. The receptionist pointed to a notice board with details about room allocation. Ah yes! There was my name against Room 3; that meant ground floor.

I was just about to move away and find Room 3 when I noticed a lady, obviously a delegate, struggling with luggage and crutches. I could tell that she wasn't best pleased about something.

I approached her; "Can I help, at all?" I asked.

She turned. "They've put me on the second floor, Room 225. The idiots know that I have difficulty with stairs and this mausoleum doesn't have a lift," she fumed.

"I'm in Room 3, ground floor. We can swap, if you like. I'll help you along there with your luggage." With that, I grabbed the heavy items and led the way to my former room. Somewhat mollified, she followed.

I dropped her bags in the middle of the room and I think she was going to offer me a 50p piece and then thought better and offered instead a rather reluctant thank you.

I think I got the better deal, for 225 was a light, airy room with a pleasant view of the river. I unloaded my few possessions and flopped onto the bed. Let's have a look at the programme; or, essentially, when do we eat?

'Buffet Get Together' at 7.00pm in main hall – come and meet your fellow delegates! With light refreshments; I don't like the sound of that, particularly the light part. Another hour to go. I'll have a wander round the place just to get my bearings.

The Ness was not always a hotel. It was probably a mansion house in Victorian times and may have some interesting nooks and crannies. With this in mind, I returned to the ground floor where anything of interest may be lurking.

That large room must have been the ballroom at one time, now presumably full of light snacks. Further along was a door labelled The Library. I decided to have a look round. I entered a gloomy chamber lighted by clefts of daylight spilling past partially drawn curtains. Various ancient-looking volumes lined the walls on dusty shelves, their leather spines staring at me with long solemn phizogs. In spite of the warmth of the day, there seemed a chill in the air. It suited the place. I examined the titles, those that I could discern under the dust and where the gold lettering was still intact.

"You are interested in books, then?" It was my acquaintance, now partially hidden in the gloom. "An unusual trait in this younger generation."

I mumbled something in reply and walked slowly along the tightly packed volumes.

"Some of these tomes are quite old," she continued, "but not to my taste. Too much hocus-pocus in them. Ancient rites and peculiar customs."

'Oh,' I thought. 'Right up Charley's street.' "I have a friend who has a deep interest in such things. He could really go to town here."

She sniffed disapprovingly.

"I must note some of these titles before I leave next week. He would be interested, I'm sure. He lives on Canna, one of the Small Islands.

"Not Sir Charles Munroe!" she exclaimed.

The 'Sir' was news to me. "The very one. I take it you know him, then?"

"Oh yes! We are old sparring partners. I've known him since our Oxford days. We were students together, but not particularly good friends. We fought a lot."

Judging by her tone (a touch of nostalgia there) I didn't really believe her. I must tease him about her when I get back. "Who shall I say I met?"

"Celia Courtley," she offered. "Time to go and meet the other goons in the ballroom. Shall we go?" and she took my arm – my escort for the evening, it seemed.

Together we entered the ballroom/conference room swirling with beards and tweeds. Everyone seemed to have arrived early save us and I expect the 'snacks' had all disappeared. We managed to salvage a couple of cheese and tomato with our rather indifferent sweet Sherry. As always in my experience, the sound waves above the cacophony of voices were taken by *Eine Kleine NachtMusik;* I wonder if Mozart wrote anything else?

I spotted Jamie Forrester, an old acquaintance, and excused myself. As I pushed through the milling crowd, I passed various plummy accents and one group in particular which was discussing the merits of the latest Porsche.

"Boy am I glad to see you, Jamie; a familiar face among all these foreigners. How are things?"

"Oh, all right, I suppose," was the gloomy reply. "I saw you come in with Her Ladyship."

"Why the doom and gloom, Jamie? You should be full of the joys of spring, even though it is autumn."

"It's tomorrow, Ken. I'm supposed to be giving a paper on my work." He picked up another insipid Sherry and drained the tiny glassful in one gulp.

"Me too. I have a presentation on the work on Canna."

He looked slightly blank, not unusual for Jamie.

"Lets get out of here and see if we can get something decent to eat; maybe a drink too," he suggested and we jostled our way to the exit.

It wasn't difficult to find what we desired; just follow the aroma and there was Chez Marco, a superior fish and chip restaurant if the sign was to be believed. We sat and were approached almost immediately. The order went back: cod and chips twice. In no time two oval platters arrived with the battered cod and lovely golden chips, nice and dry and not the usual dripping-with-fat variety.

With a couple of cokes, the feast was fast vanishing when it occurred to me that Celia Courtley would appreciate this. She too had suffered a cheese and tomato apology at the opening.

"Hey, Marco! Do you have carry-outs?"

He nodded.

"A single portion of the same again, then. I'll take it right away."

I scurried back to the Ness Hotel as soon as the order arrived and took it straight to Room 3. On my knock, the door opened, I sort of mumbled something, thrust the boxed carry-out into her hands and fled back to Marco's.

Jamie greeted me with, "For a moment, I thought you had left me with the tab," and I sat down to finish the last few chips. There seemed to be fewer than I remembered.

"Are you all ready for your presentation, tomorrow," I asked? "What is it on, your paper?"

"That's the problem, Kenny. I don't have a lot to say. I'm supposed to be in charge of the rehabilitation of the hedgehogs from Lewis, you know, the ones that were flown from the island to the mainland. But there is not a lot you can say on that. They fly them in; I release them in some woodland; that's it." He looked more than a little concerned.

I thought for a moment. "Just say: so many in a hedgerow of hawthorn, some in a hayfield border, others in a beech wood and so on. Say that you plan to return to the sites to see how they are faring."

"That's great," as he scribbled notes on a little jotter. "Anything else?"

"Hey, wait a minute. It's your project. You'll know what you've done."

"That's the problem. I can't remember where I put them."

We left it there for I wasn't going to compose his fairy-tale. I have my own to worry about. I made a mental note that this was a good place to eat and certainly better than my hotel. I am open to improvements to the latter.

On the lane back, we were waylaid by Lady Celia. "I want to thank you two for your thoughtful gesture. It was most welcome. I just hope that catering here improves over the next few days. Come into my room."

There she produced a bottle of Glenlivit, a passable single malt, and when I think about it, a local brew. We didn't object to the polystyrene cups and the rest of the evening passed quite amiably with hazy small talk.

I did notice when leaving Room 3, the raised eyebrows of the few passers-by. Perhaps it was our erratic passage.

The following day was the big one, the one when Jamie and I would be giving our 'learnéd' papers. I rose early to prepare my wits for the occasion. Gazing at my reflection from the bathroom mirror, I observed baggy eyes and wan expression, not a good omen for the afternoon session. Off to the freshness of the Highland air and a brisk walk in the morning sun.

We assembled for the plenary session in the afternoon and I could see with some satisfaction that Jamie's hangover was worse than mine. He nevertheless presented a reasonably coherent paper on hedgehogs along the lines I suggested. I did notice a group of three of the Porsche set with the plummy voices sitting giggling like a group of school kids during Jamie's address. They were going to be trouble.

Later in the afternoon, it was my turn. I stood at the lectern and, remembering the Laird's advice, I paused and look around at the assembly before starting on my paper. Partway through, the middle one of the trio gave an unconcealed yawn. I stopped in midsentence with "You there! Yes, the one yawning. Get out if you find it so boring!" The one in question turned red and tried to look small. "Yes you! Get out!" He still didn't budge so I just carried on unperturbed.

At the end of my brief paper, I received a louder than customary round of applause, an endorsement of my outburst. At the finish, Jamie came up. "What was all that about?"

"The ignorant sod sat there yawning, trying to put me off so I just thought I would give him a little dig. Expect trouble when we see them again, Jamie." We went off to collect our lukewarm coffee and chocolate digestive with some encouraging smiles on the way. "Don't get involved. Just leave them to me," I advised.

After a bit, I left the conference room to return my papers to my room. Right enough, there they were, the three of them waiting in the corridor. When they saw me, they spaced themselves across the passage essentially blocking my way. Without a break in my stride, I stepped along and stood facing the central figure, the ringleader and stood about a foot from him. "Excuse me!" No response. No movement. So I biffed him really hard - on the nose where it undoubtedly hurt. He staggered back, slide down the back wall blood trickling from his nose, a startled expression in his eyes. I strode on my way round the corner of the corridor and replaced coins to my right hand pocket. My early years living in a South Ayrshire mining village hadn't been wasted after all.

Jamie caught me up as I reached the stairs. "That's one way to get past a road block. The other two just stood there with their mouths open."

I looked at him and winked. "There's nothing like a spot of blood to knock the resistance from the opposition;" and we climbed the stairs to our respective rooms. I sagged on the bed and nursed my hand. God it was painful!

Later, I collected Jamie for the evening meal which again was rather ordinary. This calls for another visit to Marco's to sample his delightful cuisine probably a final visit; for I would be on my way back to Canna the following day.

Afterwards, I decided to have an early night. The emotional happenings of the day had drained me and my right hand was throbbing a bit. I wonder how his nose is faring?

"Well Jamie, I'm off back home tomorrow and I think I've had enough excitement for today."

I bade him goodnight and returned to my room. I was determined to have a good night's sleep; for the journey back was long.

For some time, I lay supine calling on Morpheus to swallow me up and eventually I did drop off - although not in any profound way. Irrational thoughts continually ran though my brain turning this way and that and ended up macabre, no doubt the effect of the library and its contents. Ghouls and goblins, spectres and spooks and shadows, cantraips and crypts . . . Just at my deepest point, there was a most terrible scream, a banshee I thought; although I can't say that I know what a banshee sounds like.

I sat bolt upright and I could detect movement and murmuring. I was reluctant to investigate. Nevertheless, I slipped on my dressing gown, the red silky one, sort of Noël Cowardish. Carefully, I opened my door a peep and could see and hear much movement. It was coming from downstairs. I ventured down to the ground floor and overheard someone saying; "There were three of them . . . frightening . . . with a white thing covering his face . . . no, his nose . . . Room 3 . . . yes three thugs . . . "

The three thugs were my three Porshe acquaintances, I guessed. They must have taken my room number from the notice board. The screams were from Room 3, Celia's room. I think I've seen the last of that lot of clowns; and I smiled smugly.

The following day after lunch, I was saying my farewells to Jamie and some others when we were approached by Lady Celia. "I want a word with you, young man;" she was speaking to me.

Feeling shifty, I waited for the onslaught. "I have a feeling you had a hand in last night's affair."

I shook my head and tried to look innocent while Jamie just looked puzzled; he had slept through the whole episode.

"The three ruffians burst in on me – no warning," she continued. "I was reading at the time. I just let out a scream and they fled but I think I would recognise them again."

I continued to remain silent and virtuous like. "I'm just off to catch my bus back – to Canna." I ventured, "Any message for Sir Charles?"

She snorted, stared for a moment and offered; "Oh, tell him it has been the most enjoyable conference I've attended for many a day." With that, she turned and hobbled back to the Ness Hotel.

The Fourth Dimension

They say that time is the fourth dimension. I cannot accept that; it's too glib. Take the other three, length, breadth and height. We measure them using a tape and some sort of system of units. We can move along them and back again, if we wish. The fact that time is non-reversible scuppers the idea that it can be treated in the same way as the regularly accepted dimensions. You cannot go back in time (except in your own mind) although scientists have stretched time ahead a little by tinkering with speed, an esoteric idea I can't cope with.

I feel that the confusion arises because of our methods for measuring time; they are mechanical and move linearly with a tick and a tock. Since forever, man has tried to measure time with his clocks and watches, his hourglass and sundial. The Romans with their candle and the Egyptians with their water clocks. Nowadays if you want to be super accurate, you use an atomic clock which operates on the frequency of electronic transitions in an atom (usually caesium.) Einstein reckoned that time is relative and flexible, a concept difficult to accept but I doubt if that bothered prehistoric man. What does bother me is how man anticipated the summer solstice (or the winter one, for that matter.) Did he calculate it without a knowledge of number? These ancient stone circles show an extraordinary understanding of the starry heavens. Of course in those days, they could see the stars without the distraction of fogs, bright lights and bearded loons with telescopes.

I've always been fascinated by time. Let me make it clear from the beginning; I do not collect clocks. Nor am I a horologist. Clocks collect me. I feel I must explain.

I would be quite happy to have one clock in the house but they keep landing on my doorstep and who am I to turn away an orphan timepiece. It all started with free offers, I suppose. "If you buy our three piece suite, you will be presented with a handsome mantle clock."

And so, over the years, I have accumulated several clocks. In the living room, there are 3 clocks and a lights timer; a clock and the microwave timer in the kitchen together with the central heating control; one in the entrance hall and something on the phone that I've still to fathom out. My study has a wall clock as has the computer. Going upstairs, there is a wag-at-the-wall on the landing; that's what they called them in my young days. The front bedroom has a bedside alarm which I never hear. The back bedroom has its own alarm (stopped) and a scattering of others in various drawers. Attached to a tree in the garden there is a wall-clock which used to be on the upper landing before it went defunct. This is converted to a bird feeder - the local birds now know when it is time for lunch or whatever. It still chimes on the hour – Westminster chimes, sort of.

It's not just clocks though. There are all the various watches with some sort of different history attached, mainly dire. When one of my watches breaks down, it's usually not worthwhile repairing and it gets chucked to the back of some drawer. When I was a student, I had a watch which was forever stopping and I reckoned that it needed cleaning. I duly dipped it into a beaker of acetone and all the numbers came off. Thereafter, I was the only student who was timeless; in reality, I was away ahead of my time (note the play on words!)

In a drawer somewhere I have two pocket watches which are family heirlooms. One is gold, the other silver and neither is in working order. I have probably omitted one or two – oh, there is the dashboard clock in the car.

Needless to say, none of them is at the right time, maybe a little before or perhaps after and one is deliberately 20min fast. There is a reason for this, crazy as it sounds. The clock is a pendulum one (battery really) and is what used to be called a grandmother clock. It sits on the wall just adjacent to the telly and opposite a long chaise-long. Visitors come and automatically sit on the couch facing this clock and, if by any chance they should overstay their welcome, I glance at the timepiece saying, "Is that the time!" Sometimes it works. As for all the other timepieces being out of time, I put this down to changing them all by one hour twice a year. I suppose it's something to do in the dark nights – make them darker; or if I get it right, make them lighter. I see there is some talk of giving up this practice.

Those who philosophise via the arts use time for their own ends. You can see this in Dali's creation, The Perception of Memory readily recognised for its images of melting watches. Or in music, the Dance of the Hours, was written in sound and dance by a range of composers – Poncielli for one and Delibe in Waltz of the Hours in the ballet Coppelia.

Sometimes I picture all my clocks and watches joining in – with calendars, of course – in some mad dance, a quadrille of sorts or even a jig or a reel; throwing arms in all directions and ticking convulsively to some demented tune. Must get on my composer's hat while the idea is alive. As the poet McCaig says,

I've a map of tomorrow.

When I get there

I'll look round anxiously to see

If it's out of date.

And so it goes on – we mark time by events.

To measure time mechanically must be wrong. The tick-tock merely counts how this device progresses from wind up to run down. If you think about it, how often have you endured an occasion – a lecture, say – and thought how slowly time passes? Then there are dreams – over in a flash. Those who have measured dreams using brain impulses say that a dream takes but a fraction of a second – if they are to be believed; but who are we to doubt? Perhaps you can have some thoughts on that!

Still I wonder if time varies like a piece of elastic, and whether it is really the constant parameter we assume it to be. George Mackay Brown touches on this in his novel, "Beside the Ocean of Time."

. . . *the trows (trolls) who live under the green knolls and love above all the music of men, so that they cajole young fiddlers to their courts and keep them there for fifty winters; but the young crofter with the fiddle, having drunk from their silver cup, thinks he has been among the roots and sources for half an hour, no more.*

What's on tele tonight? What can I waste my time on rather than on something useful. I pick a magazine with programmes – let's see – no! that one was last night and I can go back and look at the recording. What am I doing? I am turning back time (in a way) to review an event in the past; to watch a rerun of that past yet in no way can I alter any event in that record – or can I? I look at the recorder. "Fast forward." I can speed up time. There is the "Fast back" to give a reverse action. Had I the equipment, I could cut out chunks and rearrange the whole story. Despite that, I am not interfering with time, merely editing it.

What is all this to do with anything? My current job is concerned with time; I now work with the Space Agency (British Branch). I don't really know how I got involved with them but I suspect it was through a couple of papers I wrote for the New Scientist. They were about a fresh look at space travel and it was more with tongue in cheek than serious theories or proposals. So, here I am with the Agency.

If you examine dispassionately the current situation regarding space travel, man has only scratched the surface with his puny efforts. Certainly, he has landed on the Moon and sent various space vessels to other planets in our system. He has talked big about future plans to send men to Mars. Yet all these plans are limited by certain factors the main one being speed, velocity, momentum, call it what you will; that is, the movement of anything three dimensional is limited by the speed of light. This in turn means that if you could travel that fast, it would take you about 4 years to get to the nearest star in our galaxy. The laws of physics don't let you travel that fast – something about mass changing to energy – that is, you would go pop.

Yet here I am with the Space Agency with the task of examining the nature of the fourth dimension. It's my own fault, I suppose, after I had written that paper about the nature of time, all a lot of conjecture and that's a polite way of putting it. The way things are, the Space Agency will seize any opportunity to justify their space program (notice the American spelling) no matter how crazy the idea; and mine was crazier than most. Essentially what I had to do was find some way of harnessing the so-called time line. In this way, we could travel anywhere without the restriction of the speed of light. Anyway, that was my idea. You could call it 'away with the fairies!'

I have a nice new laboratory complete with assistant, Jenny Ryan. Actually, she is a nurse, not because of my mental state, but because of the nature of the research. There are several electronic gadgets, most of them for window dressing when I have visitors. Certainly I'll use some of them, for I do have some ultra-sensitive measurements to make, in particular time-lapse parameters. There is a large desk to make me appear important and on it there is the obligatory desktop computer. There is a smaller one for my assistant (less important) also with computer, various filing cabinets, a selection of books (mainly medical) and a secure cabinet for sensitive chemicals. One corner is taken with a chemistry workbench complete with basic analytical chemicals on a set of shelves and an array of analytical instruments such as GLC and electrophoresis. Apart from some other bits and pieces, the only unusual item is a bed, all part of the experimental procedures, as you will see.

I make these personal notes on my computer, save on a memory stick and then delete the file. Needless to say, I don't want my personal feelings exposed for all to read. It is more than my job is worth. My report to the powers-that-be is much more formal and laid out in a scientific fashion. After all, I can bluff my way just as well as the next researcher.

You may wonder too about the bed. I'm sure Jenny does too. However, it is all very scientific as you will see. It is designed to tilt in all three dimensions as well as move up and down; there are straps to hold the occupant in place and the mattress is held securely to the frame. Thus it covered all angles of dip as well as all points of the compass. The whole basis of my programme of research rests in the nature of dreams. Other investigations have shown that, in a dream, a whole lifetime can flash through a dream in an instant. I wish to find if the speed of this flash is limited by, say, the speed of light. My initial aim, then, is to try and dream! and then to control the nature of the dream.

My first problem is to induce the dream in the first place and where better to start than hallucinatory drugs, hence the secure cabinet. I had taken upon myself to be the guinea pig – without the treadmill. Jenny would inject me with the appropriate drug (in small, measured amounts) and record various parameters, blood pressure, temperature, brain reaction impulses.

I had loads of sleep over the following several weeks but no useable dreams to follow up with different bed angles. My arm was beginning to look like a junkies before we thought of inserting a catheter. Maybe I thought I would hit a dream-drug among the array of psychedelics I had available, but no such luck. We must leave these alkaloids and change direction.

"What are we trying to do here?" asked Jenny. You'll note the 'we'.

"Well, it's like this," I explained. And I started on my usual rigmarole for visitors and the like.

"Oh!" She seemed annoyed and she listened almost tapping a foot in exasperation. "You should have said. In my experience, you have to mix one of the alkaloids with alcohol. That's what happens at raves and the like."

She could have a point and so the next trial had a little Bowmore mixed in with the alkaloid. The Bowmore malt was taken by mouth, of course. And why not! I was the one taking the risk.

Believe it or not, it worked. There in my induced dream amid all the debris and almost hidden by the dross of receding patterns and distorted motifs, I could discern a line, almost a road receding into the distance. I think the success of the experiment must have been reflected in my brain impulses; for when I came round, Jenny seemed as excited as I was.

"Look at these patterns! They are almost off the oscilloscope grid," she exclaimed. We both dance round the room in our excitement, although I reckon my pirouette was somewhat erratic and alcohol related. At last I had something positive to relate to my masters.

This was one of many reports, but the first to show any realistic success. It started with the usual intro. on the background and then led to the meat:

REPORT 31: *Fourth Dimensional Analysis*

. . . *The results from the most recent experiment, show a distinct line or road that suggested further study of the use of certain alkaloid/alcohol mixtures. Such mixtures produced a defined pathway in the brain (the Ryan Effect,* I might as well give Jenny the credit*) that should prove fruitful as an access to the so-called fourth dimension. The mixture used in this experiment was an alkaloid, ketamine and 40v/v % alcohol produced by a malting process. There are different ways this project can proceed – 1) Examine alcohols from different sources to find if the Ryan Effect is common to the alcohol content or to the different water sources; 2) Examine different ways of controlling the pathway. I favour the* *latter for our main effort without losing sight of the former as a minor aspect of this project. With this in mind, I would request permission to seek out different sources of 40v/v% ethanol. Nevertheless, we intend to pursue the controlling of the pathway as our principal objective.*

Chief officer, 4D project

In spite of all the blarney, I was really quite excited about the whole project and I arranged with Jenny the delicate details involved in ordering additional alkaloids and a range of Islay malt whiskeys. We also had the important task of designing the next experiment.

A few days later, I viewed our security cabinet and our new acquisitions. I wasn't too bothered about the alkaloids. They appeared quite mundane. It was the row upon row of Islay malt whiskeys that caught the eye. The Bowmore, half empty I noticed, Bruichladdich, Ardbeg, Laphroaig,, Lagavulin and so the list goes on. The names roll off the tongue as does the amber nectar and as I gaze at the array, I decided it was only fair also to include a bottle of Jura from the neighbouring island. However, I came to the conclusion that the display was incomplete. Not for long. I purchased six whisky glasses of Edinburgh crystal.

I found too that Jenny was developing a taste for the amber liquid; for each time we ran a new test, she had a wee dram herself. Some samples had to be treated with caution, for they were about 57v/v% (that's about 100º proof.)

It was with one of these where we had our first real success. As ever after my injection plus dram I lay down and almost immediately I went into this dream, if that is what it was. I was off along this silvery route with no sensation of speed yet flying without hindrance. There was no dimension to my trip, at least no physical hindrance as I flew through any solid in my path. I think that that was the asteroid belt I left and in an instant I raced past an extremely large bulk to hover over Saturn; I recognised the rings. I seem to have reached the limit of my trip and oscillated back and forth on my rubber band umbilical .

All was blurred, unfocused and soundless. I was aware of Jenny shaking my shoulder. She seemed anxious. "Your blood pressure almost hit the ceiling – it's over 200/86. I was getting concerned."

Rather subdued, I related my experiences and then lay back to sleep for quite a period, as it happens.

The following days, I repeated the experiment with the bed turned to different points of the compass. I must be getting acclimatized to the experience for my blood pressure didn't react so drastically. However, the journey was the same each time. I had no choice but to go on the same 'mystery tour' without the mystery.

We continued the experiments altering the different variables with no changes to the result. Still no control over the route or destination. That is, until two and a half bottles of Ardbeg later, four bottles if you count Jenny's share (the Angels' share, I called it) when the passage took a different direction. The path took me to a strange sight, for there seemed to be two bright centres, almost like two suns and then I noticed a third much fainter satellite. When I return, I must search the astronomy literature for an identification. And in a blink, I was back in the laboratory.

"Jenny, Jenny," I burbled. "I've been with the stars." I loosened the retention buckles and sat upright. Jenny handed me a pick-me-up and the two of us sat at the larger desk with picture books of the stars. This was an easy one to find for it was a group nearest the Earth called Centaurus. "Was Centaurus the star they used to test the eyesight of Roman soldiers?" Jenny shook her head in despair . . . probably thought I was doolally.

"Now let's analyse the situation," I continued. "The chemical stimulants were the same as expt. 53. The angle of dip (of the bed) was altered to 43º and that was it, nothing else," I puzzled. "Have we changed anything else," I mused.

"The blood supply to the brain has increased," Jenny suggested, "and I noticed that the brain oxygen levels were up."

"Right. We'll get in a cylinder of oxygen and a face mask and try that in our next experiment," I suggested. "Oh, and don't forget the reduction valve for the cylinder."

End of personal record/ memory stick #5

* **

"He's been like this for the past 24 hours, just staring straight ahead." Jenny had brought in the project director and they were just gawping at the immobile Space Traveller. "I just can't get any reaction. He was trying out a new combination with more oxygen."

The director just seemed perplexed. "Leave it just now and we'll look at the situation in two days. You're a nurse so take over. I'll get a relief for nights."

With that, he just left her to it.

Jenny busied herself, not only with the patient but also with getting rid of the evidence, the personal memory stick #5 and the 'hard stuff' together with the personal notes on the computer. She didn't want prying eyes poking in computers or secure cupboards.

The relief nurse seemed reliable enough and no great problem. True to his word, the director returned this time with the site doctor and they stood close together mumbling to one another. They had come to a decision. The doctor produced a syringe; "A shot of adrenaline should do it." That was it, straight into the catheter.

The reaction was virtually immediate. The Space Traveller sat bolt upright, cried," Sagittarius" and flopped down, lifeless.

The Fetlar Fiddler

If you sail north from the Scottish mainland and brave the Pentland Firth, you will come across the Orkney group of islands. If you are even more adventurous and sail even further past Fair Isle, you arrive at the Shetland Islands. The island of Fetlar is one of these. It nestles under the shadow of Yell and Unst and is a mere 20 minutes sail from Toft on Shetland Mainland.

Generally, we are aware of the Shetland Islands through their association with the oil industry and the oil terminal at Sullom Voe. The time I am speaking of goes much further back when the influences were more Norse orientated than Scottish although some argue – mainly Shetlanders – that this is still the case. There is still a small thriving community living on Fetlar, because it is a good place to live. You can stretch your eyes to the horizon, listen to the endless singing of the wind and feel the breathing of the sea beneath you as you slide over its bosom to the island. Some see it as an attractive little island; others are less kind and call it bleak.

The Vikings knew Fetlar long before the Scottish Kings got their hands on it. The Norsemen thought of it as two islands joined together rather like Lewis and Harris. They even divided the island into two by erecting a stone dyke, the Funzie Girt. Of course, because of its connections, it had its quota of trolls, all part of any Norse island.

Some time ago in spite of there being much fertile soil, there was a patch of poor land which was worked by a farmer and his wife, Hjalmar and Abijah Axelsen. Life was hard for the two, for the ground was poor and most of the farm was committed to sheep and one cow. There was also a better patch for oats and some roots for their own use. However, the sea close by was a rich source of additional means. Apart from the occasional fish they managed to catch – usually mackerel and the occasional saithe – there was a multitude of shell fish of various kinds. The main crop from the sea, however, was the wealth of flotsam, mainly wood. Sometimes there was a bottle or even some rope, all useful materials to the poorer island people. Hjalmar and his wife spent much of the day collecting wood and carrying it to their fuel store for the cold and long winter months. The rest of the farm looked after itself most of the time apart from the vegetable patch and the constant demands of its weeds.

One sunny day on the beach, a flash of light caught Hjalmar's eye. As he got closer, he could see what appeared to be a half-buried coffin. He stood well back for some time inspecting it from a distance. It was fine pine and it was quarter cut, unusual in those days. "It must have come from a passing ship," he thought; "A fine piece of pine!" As he stared at it various thoughts and ideas passed through his mind. "Come look at this, Abi!" His wife ambled over and seemed troubled when she saw the object. Plucking up courage, Hjalmar edged closer when he could see that it was only the lid of the coffin lying there half-buried. Emboldened he kneeled and wiped away some of the sand suppressing a natural shudder. "I'll take it up to the house and maybe keep it to work on over the winter," he continued. "The cut of the timber will be useful for a carving job," trying to appear unconcerned; but he was still uneasy. He could see that Abijah shared the feeling – the very idea of having such an item in the house. "Och, it's OK, just a bit of wood. See! There's no coffin underneath," as he prised the lid from its sandy grave. He was picturing all sorts he could make from such a prize.

Summer drifted by, as summer days do; for Fetlar was sheltered from the westerlies by the island of Yell. The air was warm and kind and their little crop patch flourished. The coffin lid stood brooding in its amber glow in a corner of the small farmhouse and was progressively joined by other selected pieces of driftwood rescued from the nearby shore. Other less interesting items were stored in the fuel shed along with the recently dried peat. Hjalmar sighed with a certain degree of satisfaction and smiled in anticipation of an interesting winter.

The glimmer of oil lamps lit the interior of the home. The pungent smell of the burning animal oil filling every corner was the indication that winter was finally here. Hjalmar had assembled his bits and pieces and his tools, such as they were. His knife and axe were keen and sharp after some work with his whittling stone and he had borrowed a saw from neighbour Harald for a short period.

Night after night he worked on the project using the saw to cut a rough shape. Some of the wood he split with the axe before smoothing the timber with broken glass shards from a bottle gleaned from the shore. The rest was up to his skill with the trusty knife.

Little by little the idea took shape and Abijah smiled when she recognised that shape. Hjal had a glue-pot made from animal bones and came the time when the bits and pieces had to be stuck together, with a bit of fitting here and there. He remembered what his grandfather had told him many years previous; for he in his time had made many similar. "The table must be quarter cut pine and the back should be some sort of hardwood like elm. Strengthen the table with a block and place a pillar between the table and the back to spread the sound throughout the sound box – oh, and don't forget to put your mark on the inside!" Yes! Hjalmar was making a fiddle.

Over the following months the instrument took shape. Hjalmar started by making the body shape with clay from the hillside. The curves and the back were stuck and set with animal glue in the best tradition. He carefully removed this skeleton from its clay mould and spliced a stock of elm to the end. Now was the exciting job of fitting and gluing the table on top. As the fingerboard, another slice of hardwood was glued to the stock hanging over the table. A peg head of four holes topped the end to complete the instrument – well almost. Pegs were fitted to the head but were of little consequence, for what was he going to use as strings.

"Abi, what am I going to do about strings for my instrument?" he asked; and he thought for a bit.

"Why not use a thairm that I was keeping soaked in a bowl of water," she replied. "I was going to make a haggis with it, but we'll have a mealy pudding instead."

At that, Hjalmar brightened up and immediately started experimenting eventually producing a sort of string. "This is going to be trickier than I thought." After much more experimenting and twisting of sheep gut, he produced a much finer version that was more presentable. It would probably do. After further scraping with a glass edge, he searched for a piece of beeswax he thought he had stashed away for just this sort of use. He rubbed this into the wood and polished and rubbed and polished and rubbed until it glowed with a deep amber. With strings fixed to a tailpiece, the fiddle fair hummed in anticipation as the strings tightened.

The bow was going to be a problem, though. Hjalmar had collected the remains of a willow tree and a withy from this would be the stick when bent in a bow shape. But what about the hair? His grandfather had said that it should be from a horses tail, but there are no horses on Shetland. Neighbour Harald had a pony; he would ask him for some of its tail when he returned the borrowed saw. Meantime, he just impatiently plucked away at the strings. "That's another thing. How should I tune the strings? Granda' said something about making the left-most string sound doh and its neighbour should be tuned to soh. Then you call that one doh and tune the next to soh and so on till all four are tuned – whatever all that means. I'll find out at the Island's New Year Festival, Up Helly Aa. It's just a couple of weeks away."

In January, the Festival arrived and all the islanders zeroed in on Dougie's farm at Ulsta. After the usual side shows and exhibitions of jam, the Festival Bonfire was lit – just a plain ordinary bonfire, not like the la-di-da one in Lerwick. The old barn served as a shelter for the main activity of the evening, eating and dancing to the two fiddles of Ali and Jan. And all night Hjalmar sat and gazed at their dexterity and listened to the tunes and learned from the fiddlers. Slow sentimental airs – the Silvery Voe – the jigs and the reels and the tunes – some familiar, some not – and Hjalmar sat and drank it all in; while Abijah smiled and observed and understood. At one point, Hjalmar had a brief and intense conversation with fiddler Ali. He found that if he could sing the lowest note he could manage, Ali identified it as a D, the same as the third string; and yes, his grandfather had been right about the mode of tuning. And still Abijah smiled.

Dawn came late, almost not at all. The couple walked home in the half light of the Northern Isles' winter. Not much was said. Hjalmar was lost in his fiddle thoughts. Abjilah was thinking of all the lost dancing for the sake of Hjal's latest obsession but said little. The thought of the desecrated coffin lid still bothered her – and still she said little. Back home, she prepared some Atholl Brose to chase away those winter woes.

After a brief turn around the farm and the usual check of winter jobs – fodder for the livestock, a survey of the roof thatch, fuel for the evening hours – Hjalmar moved into the main house. There was Abjilah staring into space; she no longer smiled. "What troubles you, Abi? Is it the coffin lid? It's only a piece of pine, nothing to be bothered about." She nodded but said nothing.

Hjalmar spent most of the evenings getting to know his instrument, to put into use all he had learned at the Festival. He held the fiddle between his knees and stroked the bow across its strings. Strangely enough, the sound was not too bad, indeed it was quite pleasant just to sit there and listen. Before long, Abjilah got accustomed to the Hjal's music making and her apprehension faded into the past. Indeed, after a time she got to her feet and danced a few steps to the reels and jigs. Before long, they would both go outside where there was more room and have a little ceilidh of their own.

The notes of the coffin fiddle did not go unnoticed. Little figures peeped out from stone wall and mowdy hillocks, their limbs twitching to the rhythms. Little green eyes gleamed with delight as the trolls had their own version of a ceilidh with legs and arms in all directions. They ignored the couple and went their own way.

This continued night after night, as nights grew shorter; and already it was spring with their lone hawthorn threatened to burst into blossom. It stood there, all oxters and elbows, bowing to the east away from the chill of the wind. Come near the end of April it burst into full bloom in time for Beltane.

That evening as soon as the sun went down, out came the fiddle, out came Hjalmar and Abjilah, out came the trolls. The tuning done, the notes from the fiddle rang clearly round the green hills – now almost black – and before long, as on other evenings, all joined in the jigs and reels; Abjilah, trolls and other creatures of the island left their dens and shelters, their haunts, dugouts and other shelters. After all, it was Beltane and all must celebrate and bid farewell to winter.

Round and round they pranced kicking their legs high in the air in exuberant ecstasy. All night long the trolls danced in three almost-touching circles, birling round with legs and arms and beards flailing the air, shrieks of elation echoing through the shadows. The beat of the fiddle increased, the jigs and the reels grew more frenetic; the fiddler's fingers raced over the strings with immense ferocity; the whole jamboree seemed taken over by some uninvited presence. As the dance quickened, a group of the trolls broke away from the others and formed a berserk circle around the farmer and his wife. They whirled widdershins round and round kicking the ground now and then with their right foot sending showers of peat towards the two. All at once, this circle started singing, a high and slow obligato to the fiddler's tune, a sort of bellow in octaves.

Every time they clomped their right foot thrice, the harmony changed and the mood darkened; the wailing turned sinister. The playing and the tunes and the dancing became more and more frenzied and none noticed the fleet of time until the morning sun lipped the edge of Funzie. By then it was too late. With a great flash and thunderclap, the whole scene was petrified, transfixed, turned to stone. The fiddle alone lay there unchanged until the ravages of time devoured it.

* * *

If you happen to visit the Shetland Island of Fetlar today, you will find near the middle of the island three stone circles of petrified trolls at a place called *Fiddler's Crus.* At a short distance stand two stones surrounded by another stone circle containing an earth circle, the result of the earth-kicking dance. This place is called *Hjaltadans* (Limping Dance).

www.ingramcontent.com/pod-product-compliance
Lightning Source LLC
LaVergne TN
LVHW012042160826
845678LV00014B/2677

* 9 7 8 0 9 5 0 8 2 3 8 1 2 *